D0169822

THE RED BOOK

Meaghan Delahunt

GRANTA

Granta Publications, 12 Addison Avenue, London W11 4QR

First published in Great Britain by Granta Books, 2008
This paperback edition published by Granta Books, 2009

A CIP catalogue record for this book
is available from the British Library.

1 3 5 7 9 10 8 6 4 2

ISBN 978 1 84708 063 9

Typeset by M Rules

Printed and bound in the UK by
CPI Bookmarque, Croydon

Mixed Sources
Product group from well-managed
forests and other controlled sources
www.fsc.org   Cert no. TT-COC-002227
© 1996 Forest Stewardship Council
FSC

For Francis

She chooses the photographs, places them in an album and binds them in red fabric. The photographs speak of India, of different people and places; they span continents and time. To touch an album is to put it back into motion; to turn the pages is an ongoing story.

DELHI

A Sikh man and his family. A Western woman next to them with two camera bags at her feet. The shadow of the photographer, a young boy, extends along the ground.

New Delhi, India, December 2003

FRANÇOISE

It began with a photograph. The sound and the feel of it. Raghu Rai's photo of the child in the dirt. This is what led me to India.

I'd first seen it in a newspaper. It was taken in Bhopal, in 1984, just hours after the gas disaster. In other photographs, Rai caught the pyramid of bodies in the streets and the orphan-look of the survivors. The tank at Union Carbide where the chain reaction started. But it was this shot which stayed with me. I turned the page and the child's face looked up – like a pale moon buried in the earth – its opaque eyes open, an adult hand caressing its forehead. Sometimes you see an image which stops your breath, which calls out the terror and beauty and pain of the world. Sometimes you see an image which hints at your future, which sets you on your path.

Almost twenty years later I'd come here for Raghu Rai's exhibition. I'd stay a few weeks and then go to Bhopal for a residency, to work on an international project.

I'd come here to make my own photographs.

I woke up as the plane dipped over Indira Gandhi airport. When I opened my eyes the lights of Delhi tinkled below: blue and orange and green, like rows of glass bangles.

In the arrivals hall the crowds reached forward with placards and nameboards and the air pressed down. There was a rush for trolleys. An American started shouting, pushing, lunging for a trolley, but someone beat him to it. The man erupted, 'I'm a visitor to your country for Chrissakes!' When extra trolleys arrived, Indian families got in first with strategically placed relatives at doors and exits. 'Is this how you treat visitors?' The man, still shouting. At that moment, two airport attendants saw me standing alone. 'Soon,' they called to me, ignoring the man. 'Soon, madam, be ready!' They wheeled more trolleys through and the attendants urged me forward. The American and I both reached for the same one. I stumbled back as he kicked out like a toddler, catching my shin. 'It's mine,' he shouted to his wife, triumphant now, pushing back through the crowds with his elbows.

I cursed after him, rubbing my leg. An airport attendant rolled his eyes and smiled. 'You must be knowing this,' he said, pointing over at the man and his wife. 'Madam, he won't be lasting a week.'

My first time in Delhi and I was pulled under by the press of colour and sound. This was a relief because for months now when I'd tried to work, when I'd been out with the camera, the world had seemed bleached and silent, as if I maybe no longer knew how to listen.

It was good to get out of the heat of the airport away from the crowds with their nameboards and placards. To pay the fixed price for the government taxi and to be gone out into the night, into the new, away from myself. To be absorbed by the streets where the membrane between public and private dissolved. It was a full moon and everything lit up as we crossed the city. Neon Coca

Cola and Bollywood billboards. McDonalds and Barista coffee. Advertisements for cellphones. Beyond this, through the dust and the lights, there was this other world. Through the ornate trucks and taxis and the blare of horns I could see people on the median strips, shadowing the ground with limbs like twigs. Some slept, some rested in their rickshaws. But some were not sleeping. Some lay shrouded, as if already dead.

In my mind, I framed all the shots I didn't take. All the shadows and shiftings of the city at night.

'Which number?' the driver asked as the taxi slowed under a railway bridge and pulled to a stop at the edge of a small park.

I took a scrap of paper from my pocket and looked again at the address of the guesthouse. 'Four,' I said.

'Char.' He nodded. Then the driver got out of the car, looked up at the CCTV camera and spoke to the guard inside the booth. 'Char,' he repeated. The guard pointed through to a large white house on the corner and opened the gates.

It was well after midnight. Another security guard unlocked the front gate and rang a bell, and a tiny boy, maybe fifteen, opened the wire door and the door behind that and took my luggage upstairs. He padded ahead in his bare feet and the house was hushed and quiet, the air was heavy with incense, and I saw that all the mirrors were covered.

The next morning at breakfast, I met the family. The man of the house was at the table, the *Hindustan Times* spread open in front of him. An elderly woman was reading the *Times of India*. Another woman, handsome, maybe around sixty, a silver streak in her dark hair, was giving orders to the servant boy. As I walked in the man stood up with difficulty, leant on his stick and shook my hand. He introduced himself as Surjit Singh. He turned to introduce his wife Aruna and then his mother, Mrs Singh. 'She's deaf,' he said, indicating his mother. 'She's eighty-eight years old. You'll have to speak loudly.' The servant boy's name was Jigme.

Aruna smiled and asked me what I would like for breakfast. She passed me fruit salad and Jigme poured the chai.

Old Mrs Singh turned to me and said loudly and brightly, 'You are a photographer?'

'Yes,' I said.

'You are from Australia?'

'That's right.'

'Yes?' She cupped her right hand around her right ear.

'Yes, I am,' I repeated.

'How wonderful,' she said.

'Yes.' I nodded, smiling. 'I guess so.'

'But where is your husband?' she asked. 'And your children?'

'No husband.' I smiled again and shrugged. 'No children.'

'No?' She looked at me to make sure she'd heard correctly. 'No.'

'But this is sad!'

'Not for me,' I laughed. Then I saw the expression on her face.

'Mummy,' said Aruna. 'Perhaps you would like . . .'

But old Mrs Singh wouldn't be put off. She stared hard at me. 'But you are a good-looking girl! And a photographer?' she repeated, as if she couldn't quite believe it.

'That's right.'

'But no husband.' She shook her head and turned away, dismissing me, and reached for a chapatti.

'And what will you photograph?' asked Aruna, with a quick glance at her mother-in-law. 'While you are here?'

'Well . . .' I was happy to change the subject. 'I'm going to Bhopal soon, for a residency . . .'

'Bhopal?' Surjit cut in.

'Yes. Next year is the twentieth anniversary . . .'

'You foreigners.' Surjit raised his eyebrows. 'So focused on our disasters.'

'Not only disasters,' I said a little defensive. 'Other things . . .'

'Other things?'

'Well, art . . . Buddhism . . . history . . .'

'Buddhism?' Surjit interjected. 'But this is a Hindu country!'

'That may be, but . . .'

'Ahh, these Western women!' Surjit Singh took a leather pill-box from the side table, opened it and called for water. He slipped some pills into his mouth and swallowed loudly. 'They go to the Himalayas – let me tell you – they fall in love with Sherpas and monks. They marry them. They take them back home. Then abandon them.' He said this with a grave voice and complete authority. 'Be careful,' he said, shaking a finger at me. 'You might not come back.'

I said, a little too sharply, 'I'm not looking for a Sherpa or a monk.'

'Of course not,' said Aruna, giving her husband a look.

❁

Aruna was a Vashtu expert. She combined Vashtu with a little feng shui and Western interior design. She arranged small vases of bamboo and green-and-gold mirrors for wealthy clients. She placed wind chimes and laughing-Buddha statues in the correct corners. She was very successful.

In the main hall there was a photograph of Surjit as a young dark-haired child. His hair long and glossy and scraped back in a low ponytail, the fashion for Sikh boys at the time. I said to Aruna, 'Surjit looks so sad there . . .'

'He's had a sad life,' Aruna said. 'A mother who didn't want him and a father who died early. Then they lost all their wealth' – she pronounced it *velt* – at Partition.'

She went on, 'He married me – a Hindu. His mother made life difficult.' She ran a finger down the glass of the photograph, then looked over at the portrait of herself as a young bride. 'The houseboys must come and dust,' she said. 'It's been far too long.'

Old Mrs Singh exerted a strange yellow pull. I could feel it, though she rarely ventured from her room. When I asked Aruna about her she whispered, 'She's always been difficult. She had Surjit when she was still a child herself. Resented him. For many years, my mother-in-law never spoke to me. For many years she only sent messages through her relatives or the servants.'

The servants were a regular topic of conversation. It gave me a lens on this whole other world. The hidden world of anticipating needs; of wary observation; of intricate looking. Of the domestics' steady gaze and the family observing the domestics. Layers of watching. I became alert to every nuance and gesture.

'The domestics steal. That's the truth of it,' Surjit said on my second morning as I admired a small statue locked in a glass cabinet. 'I must keep everything locked. They drop things or they steal. One or the other. They have no concept of value. Can you imagine?'

'No,' I said.

Surjit was seventy-four now, bent with arthritis. Every movement pained him. But inside himself he was still a young Prince of the Punjab, presiding over vast tracts of land, heir to three palaces, employing over one hundred servants.

Each morning Jigme, the bright, slight Nepalese boy with the one bad eye and bad leg, took mustard oil heated in a basin of water and massaged Surjit's legs and arms. He laid blanched almonds on a small patterned plate. He warmed some milk mixed with six cloves of crushed garlic. 'He's back to his old regime. From twenty years ago,' said Aruna. 'But now, you see, the pain has spread to his legs and feet.'

Surjit clicked his tongue and turned to me. 'Remember this, Françoise, domestics are like animals. Like dogs and horses. If you show weakness, they will use it against you. My wife doesn't understand. She comes from a family of teachers – they have no idea. Even our domestics tell me, "She cannot run a house." Aruna always ends up subservient to the servants.'

'But we had a very good boy, once,' said Aruna. 'He saved us . . .'

'Your parents saved us.' Surjit's voice rose.

'Saved you?'

'From the mobs. But according to my wife we were saved by our boy. Such nonsense! It was after Indira – Sikh bodyguards killed Indira Gandhi – and after, the mobs came and burnt many

Sikh homes . . . retaliation . . . right here even.' He paused. 'Here, even, in this colony . . .'

'And our boy stood up to them.'

'Ahh, but without your parents behind the gate, supporting him . . . who knows?'

I listened and nodded but something in my face made Surjit sit up. He turned to me.

'This may seem strange to you, I know.'

I smiled and shrugged. 'Well – where I come from, we don't have servants.'

'But you used to!' he said, as his hands thumped the table. 'Your culture lost the art.'

I couldn't resist. 'That was never my culture . . .'

'Oh?' said Surjit. 'And in Australia? What *was* your culture?' He was amused. 'What line was your father in?'

'Post Office.'

'Director?' he asked.

'Delivery.'

Surjit sat back and smiled. I could see that my answer pleased him enormously. 'Oh,' he said. 'After Lahore, I was in tea.'

I stayed in Delhi for over a month.

I developed my own routine. Before breakfast I'd walk around the colony in the cool of early morning. For the first week I didn't take any photographs. In a new place it always took a while to accustom the eye, this was something I'd learnt. It takes a long time to train yourself to really see properly. It's a lifetime apprenticeship. To practise seeing every day, without the camera.

On good days, when I was out looking, patterns emerged. Sometimes it was cheekbones or buildings with vivid faces. Sometimes it was a gesture or the way people walked. Other days, nothing sung out.

But I'd learnt through experience that I could wait and that I could perservere.

The colony was a maze of old and new areas, marked by signs in non-alphabetical order. I'd turn right at the front gate for a lap around M block into H block, past the free homeopathic clinic with the incense spilling out through the open doors; past an old woman heating an iron on a slab under a shade tree, then into the small park, already full of big matriarchs and their plump sons, doing one lap after another, before the real heat of the day set in.

It was like a symphony, this walking. I could feel myself easing into this life here; the bright puzzle of framing what I heard. It was always a puzzle because the world is in colour and it seems so loud and raw. Orange has the woody tones of a marimba. Certain words taste gold or caramel. We're all born like this – synaesthesic, hearing colours, seeing sounds – or so the story goes. Some of us stay that way. Because of this I've always been drawn to black-and-white. It's been my way of negotiating things.

This way of seeing affects my work. All people, objects and places have a special sound and texture. India, for example, is red. Tuesday is a green day. Everything chords through me. It's what I've become known for: black-and-white photos with the *feel* of colour. Green panels and a blue sky and gold shadows on wood. You can hear it all in the shadings but there are no colours in my photographs. There's just the feel of something missing, the fabric of something absent, something long gone.

And the camera always clicks turquoise – my favourite sound.

○

After that first week, after my eye became accustomed, I roamed the streets with the camera, my old Olympus OM10. Most days I tried to avoid the obvious – the loin-clothed sadhu with the cellphone; the torn filmi poster and the limbless beggar; the slum children caught in the windows of a limousine. All the visual clichés of modern India. They were hard to avoid. On the crowded Delhi streets, I kept my two small camera bags balanced on my shoulders, too wary to place them on the ground. Every time I stopped, a crowd of men and boys would gather, curious, jostling, to look at the firangi woman taking photos.

In this busy city I was struck by people, places, things, at times when they were peeled back or when they were still. All the shots were blurred and indistinct. Part-glimpses of when I was waiting for another self or mood to take form, to take shape. People poised in a gap in the traffic. How best to photograph the gap? The worn sole of a chappal as a person ran across; a man, hand around a metal cup – the hand and cup disappearing through a doorway.

I've always been interested in fragments. How a fraction reveals or betrays, says something about the whole person. What can we tell from hands and feet, from cheekbones and clavicles? I'm interested in how other photographers do it.

In De Carava's photos of the '63 Washington March we see ankles, the hem of a skirt, the feet trawling the dust. The shoes and ankles of a woman dragged away by the police. We feel we know the woman.

Over time, I've learnt to sense the whole from its parts: an intuitive feel of how the thing could come together. Nearly all my portraits are fragmented.

After years of looking, I've learnt to see without the camera. The equipment is only part of it. A good photograph is about feeling, above all. I have my old Olympus and I always buy the best lens I can afford. I've learnt to slip through and press myself flat, get out of my own way, which has always been to my advantage. Because I want the people in my photographs to tell their own stories; to be the narrators of their own lives.

A good photograph must have a sense of inevitability about it, as if there's no other way it could have been arranged, or taken.

Up ahead, a truck painted Klein blue stopped at an intersection. In the back of the truck there were at least a dozen workers including a few women. One man held a large black umbrella over the other men to shield them from the sun. The women hooked their saris over their heads. I leant out of the taxi window and caught the rounded shapes and the hands full of fabric as the truck turned the corner.

The driver in his immaculate Maruti kept talking, non-stop. He *owned* this car, he told me. There was a distinction between an Ambassador taxi and his own superior service. He was a *driver*, he said, not an everyday taxi-wallah. Yes, I reassured him, I understood. Not taking my eyes from the lives outside the window.

The taxi stopped outside a small art gallery. It was the Raghu Rai exhibition, the Bhopal photographs. The first set was taken in 1984 just after the gas disaster. The next, seventeen years later when he returned to see the survivors. Black-and-white shots of open doors and vacant houses and occupants who never returned. There was a photograph of a man carrying his dead wife over his shoulder. Another in a graveyard, a man pointing to his heart. Then the iconic photograph I remembered. The face which had drawn me here, which had made me want to be a photographer. The shot of the unknown child, the burial of the child in the dirt, an adult hand over its forehead, its clouded eyes open. I stood in front of this photograph, filled with its terrible beauty and made sketches in my notebook.

At dinner that night, I told Surjit and Aruna about the exhibition.

'So many people died,' said Aruna. 'And still dying.' She shook her head. 'We had a boy once – the good boy I told you about – his family . . .'

'You foreigners,' Surjit interrupted her. 'I must repeat. So focused on our disasters.' He adjusted his turban before reaching for the dhal. 'But many in Bhopal were Muslim and this was the real problem. They breed like rabbits and when troubles come – they cannot look after their own.'

I asked Surjit if he had any photographs from his time in Lahore, the days in Punjab.

'I do,' he said in a heavy tone. 'But they're in leather albums, locked the almirah. They used to be in my mother's room, but one day I see them all over the floor. "Is *this* how you see our heritage? Is *this* how you remember my father? Something for the floor, only?" My mother has no idea. And so, one day I took them from her room.' He paused. 'She doesn't deserve such photographs.' Instead, he showed me old prints of his life on the tea plantations in Assam, in Bhutan. Sepia-tinted prints of cane furniture and wide verandahs, of servants in formal dress.

Then Aruna came in with her guest book, her own album, full of signatures and comments. 'Remember to sign,' she said, opening the book to show me. At the back of the guest book was an envelope full of photographs. 'People who worked here. People who stayed here,' she said. Two photographs fell out onto the floor. 'Oh my,' she said, as she bent down, turned them over, held them out for me to see. One of the photos showed a young domestic standing in front of the house. 'He was the one,' she said sadly. 'The one who saved us. The one who had to leave . . .' The other showed a young traveller with his ruck-sack. 'Oh my.' She shook her head. 'From so long ago.'

A young man stares at the camera. There is a dark stain visible on one cheek; the other side of his face is in shadow. He is barefoot and carries a bundle of washing tied with string.

New Delhi, December 1984

NAGA

I'd wake up early, lie still and listen for Memsahib. She always woke early. Then I'd unlock the door, slide the metal latch and go out onto the barsati roof. Breathe in the cool of the morning, before the day began. Lean on the balcony and wave to Nakul across the street. He'd wave back; a neem brush in one hand, scraping his teeth.

I'd look down into the street, and catch the first of the sun. Already the workmen were there. These past weeks I'd hear their calls and every morning I watched them with the bamboo frames and bits of wire. Two men lifted sledgehammers and another man in grey dhoti and vest carried the stones away. Balancing the stones on his head – wound round with orange cloth – balancing down a wood ramp to a wheelbarrow. Families sat around kerosene stoves in empty corners of the building. Dust floated down as the upper floors fell. After this house they'd move onto the next house and the next. Living where they worked.

New homes to replace those burnt down. New homes for the Sikhs still left.

I'd watch sweepers shift dust into gutters and handcarts. In summer they'd start early. It was a haze of triangle brushes and dirt.

I'd fill the basin from the tap at the edge of the barsati roof; splash my face, lift my dhoti, always like this. Then the neem bark for my teeth. Then I'd sit for some minutes praying to Buddha Amitabha, praying for this day. After, I'd stand up; reach for yesterday's washing from the line. I'd fold the starch-stiff clothes and tie with string for the press-walli. Late mornings, in M block, under the shade tree, she'd steady her heavy iron on a concrete slab and I'd take the clothes to her. Afternoons she'd move to H block, to another concrete slab under another tree.

I dressed in the old clothes of Memsahib's foreign guests. Clothes left behind. Always, I wore too-long trousers. I'd reach for a clean T-shirt: *New York, New York*. I'd mouth the words. I'd open an American book left in the guestroom. This is how I taught myself English. First, from the foreigners on Annapurna. From how they spoke. Later, from Memsahib's foreign guests. From what they left behind. Westerners always leave something. 'He's quick,' I'd hear them say to Memsahib. 'So bright. He should have lessons!' And Memsahib would smile to herself and turn away. 'Why, to have lessons?' Yet outside our colony, across the streets, there were the banners in English: *Educate your domestic help*. Every morning I'd walk under these banners to go to the market, to cross the park to Mother Dairy for milk along with a hundred others. But I was the only domestic who knew what the words meant. Who could read the promise of these words.

I learnt also from Sahib's books. All the books shut behind glass. 'Leather-cover books, not for reading, for collecting only,' said Sahib. I'd take these books out for dusting: *Sherlock Holmes*, Agatha Christie, *Encyclopaedia Brittanica*. These books with stories of cold places and rain, pale food and pale people. And then

Sahib's favourite book, the only book I ever saw him open, the one I was not allowed to dust: *Glory Days of Punjab.*

I'd walk down into the house with the sun-dried clothes. I'd hear Memsahib's soft steps. 'Namaste,' she'd smile in that sad way as she passed. 'Namaste, Memsahib,' my eyes low.

Each morning Memsahib entered her workroom and I'd follow her. My task was to straighten the wall mirror, to bring the rollers in the plastic box from the dresser. She'd take two, frown at her reflection and put the rollers at the crown of her black hair. Then she'd ask me for curd, one teaspoon only in a small bowl, and she'd mix the curd with the clay and oil she kept in bottles. I'd slide the door shut. She'd sit for ten minutes with the face mask, with the rollers, eyes closed. It was her alone time: away from Sahib, away from the old Memsahib, away from her clients and foreign guests.

After ten minutes I'd hear taps, water splashing. She'd come out and sometimes just under the chin, I'd see traces of clay.

Then I had to work quickly. The day would begin. I'd crush six garlic cloves and boil milk for Sahib's medicine. I'd put seven blanched almonds on a plate. Then the milk and the almonds on a tray. Under one arm, I'd put the *Hindustan Times.* Under the other, the *Times of India.* I'd go up carefully, balancing the tray and the papers and knock at his door. 'Hahn?' he'd call. Then repeat in English. 'Yes?' Loudly, his voice. 'Sardarji,' I'd say. 'Medicine.' I'd worry his voice would wake old Memsahib. I'd place the *Times* outside her door, listen, but no sound. Again, I'd knock at Sahib's door and enter. He'd lie in bed, one arm across his face, shielding himself from the day. I'd open the curtains. Without a word, I'd place the tray near his bed, and walk downstairs to heat the bottle of mustard oil in a pan of water.

When the water boiled, I'd test the heat of the mustard oil with my finger and turn the gas off. I'd leave the oil to cool for two minutes. Again I'd climb upstairs with the tray and the warm mustard oil. I'd set the oil down on a side table carved like an elephant next to Sahib – on top of the bed now in vest and shorts. He was a big, solid man, maybe fifty-five years old. He held his arms at his side, straight as a pole. I'd rub the mustard oil between my palms. He'd lift first one arm and then another. Still no words. I'd knead his arms from wrist to shoulder working the warm oil into his skin. Sometimes he pulled back with the pain and I'd smell the milk and garlic on his breath.

It would be a bad day if his knuckles and wrists were tight, if already the fingers had swelled. After twenty minutes, 'Bas?' I'd ask. 'Bas,' he'd say, turning away from me. Sometimes it was a test. His not looking, his not speaking. 'I know servants,' he said on my first day. 'There is no respect.' He sensed it from me. But I'd bow to him and walk down to the kitchen to wash the oil from my hands. I'd check if the old Memsahib was awake as I passed her door. I'd look for the edge of her pink dressing gown, the beaded slipper, the heavy-veined foot. The sound of pages turning. I'd wait for her call for chai.

Breakfast: I must prepare coffee, toast and eggs for the Sahib; chai for Old Memsahib. I must cook porridge, chop fruit, spoon curd for the foreign guests. I had to learn these foreign guests. To watch them closely. Observe their habits and their needs, their likes and wants. To be one step ahead. To know when to refill the water jugs. When to give fresh towels, to give paper for their toilet. To give tea, milk, and sugar – all separate – for the Britishers. To give coffee for the Americans. These foreign guests. They all watched me, watching them.

When breakfast was done I'd put old newspapers down, fill the metal plates and sit with Bisu on the kitchen floor. And again at night on the floor with the kerosene lamp. Sahib would insist, 'Why waste electricity?' Always, the lights were off for the domestics. Even in winter, there was no fire for us in the barsati. Sahib would give us old immersion rods to stand in buckets, to heat the water. But in December and January it was too cold; there was too much work, no time to stand out on the barsati roof, waiting for the water to heat.

Since October, late afternoon, after lunch, I am allowed to sleep for one hour on the kitchen floor. It is my privilege since the mob time. Since the time of Indiraji's death and Delhi on fire. Since the men with sticks and torches. We could hear the running, the screams of the women. We locked the gates, shut the lights, made the house dark. I called to Sahib and Memsahib – 'Stay back.' I called to Bisu – 'Stay back.' I could hear the running and the angry calls. I was afraid for the Sahib and the Memsahib.

I was not afraid for myself. I stood alone out on the pavement, tensed and waiting. Flexing my fingers, shifting from foot to foot. Full of anticipation. If someone has anger, they will invite anger in. They will go looking. They will attract it, always blaming, fighting, until they understand. That night, it was my own anger I was seeing. There was no escape. Those men were a mirror and after it was over I was faced with my own reflection.

'No Sikhs here.' My voice unsteady. Memsahib's parents behind the gates holding up the wooden Ganesha. I stood to face the crowd with their petrol and their rags, as they flamed the house across the street. 'No Sikhs here!' I called again as the men came close. They came with bicycle chains and torches, red eyes and fists high. They made a circle, their breath heavy, and then they saw my face, saw the silver prayer wheel at my neck, saw the statue of Ganesha, the old Hindus behind the gate. There was a murmur. The crowd paused. I stood very still, as if facing a mad dog. Then an explosion at the end of the street. A boy cried out and the crowd ran towards the sound. The crowd moved on as one person.

Inside, Sahib and Memsahib still pressed behind the door. Old Memsahib behind the almirah. 'So brave,' Memsahib said later. 'We must thank you.' But Sahib didn't say. Sahib never said. Upstairs, when the mob had left, the old Memsahib called for chai. Sahib ordered dusting, cleaning, for the rugs to be beaten. Everything must be cleaned, he said. I saw him pour his own drink – his hands shook – and then he went upstairs to stand a long time looking out over the colony.

That night, and every night, Memsahib put covers on the mirrors, to confuse ghosts and deter demons. But in this house – in this world – I wanted to say, ghosts and demons were real: always walking, shouting, and keeping silent. All torches and fists and frustrations. Why cover the mirrors?

Before I went to sleep, I hit my fists against the charpoy.

For three days there was a curfew, police and army on the streets. Then all was quiet in our colony. I walked across the park to Mother Dairy. There were empty spaces at the end of the street. A burnt-out car. The smoke smell and the ashes still hot. I walked the same route as always. I turned left, out of the colony past the girls' secondary school. The school was shut;

there was a notice on the gate. I walked past the veg-wallah's cart. I always stopped there to look, and sometimes to buy for Memsahib. To get small purple eggplant or pink carrots, to get tomatoes and spinach. The veg-wallah was there, cutting the cabbage with a big heavy slicer balanced at the rim of the cart. Thin domestics grouped around him like always, holding their rupees up. I walked past the huge pigs snuffling the garbage heap on the corner and the pariah dogs edging round the pigs. I walked past the flower stall, a young boy asleep on a sheet of cardboard next to it. I turned right again, past the house of the Tibetans – eight children and a mother – camped in an old house with no windows. The colony wanted them gone. All the neighbours agreed, except for Sahib and Memsahib. My employers had their principles. They believed in kindness to strangers. They believed in good works and karma, they said. 'No one knows how they came here, or why they are still staying. But they are poor people. We must help.' They were the only poor family in the street and often I would take veg to them left over from our kitchen. Or Memsahib would save pieces of soap tied in cloth to give them for washing. I would take old clothes from the foreign guests. Sahib also gave his old clothes. But when I went past that morning, four days after the mobs, that house was no more and the family were gone.

I walked on and waited outside the park railings. Each morning at this time a leper would pass, pushing himself in a handcart of old bicycle parts, the right leg stump shorter than the left, the right hand turning the handle. He knew everything in this colony. But no, he said. He had no news of this family. Under the bridge, the Dalit children were back with their blond dirty hair, playing with old wheels and rubber tyres, balancing the wheels with sticks. There were cycle rickshaws and autos and a bent man on a bicycle carrying a basket of brooms. Everything seemed almost as normal. The buses went past; the rear mirrors scraped the park fence. The paan seller returned. I watched him set up with his betel nut, newspaper and green leaves. I asked him about the family.

'Many people got caught,' he said. 'A mob is a mob.'

'But they were not Sikhs.'

'They were different.' He shrugged. 'A mob is a mob.'

I went back to tell Memsahib.

A week later at dinner, the talk was still of Indira Gandhi and the riots. There was a foreign guest, a Britisher, who had returned from a scientific mission in Tibet.

'Our boy is Tibetan,' said Memsahib, nodding at me as I came through from the kitchen with a tray of kulfi and chai. 'His family. They escaped and he was born in Nepal.' She smiled at me.

'Tibet?' said the Britisher, reaching over for more sugar. 'It's changing. Tell your family that.' He muttered to himself, 'And it had to change. So damn feudal.' He sighed and looked up at me then, speaking very slowly so that I would understand.

'Dalai Lama? You know Dalai Lama?'

'Hahnji,' I said. 'Yes.'

'Well, he's a fool. The Chinese run rings . . . he lets them walk all over . . . what the hell, if he'd only fight back . . .'

'To fight is not our way.' I heard the words from my mouth. English words. Memsahib and Sahib looked up.

'Ah. But it was your way. Once. The Tibetans were warriors. Fought wars. They were fighters.' He held his hand up. 'I know, I know. Don't tell me. I know all about karma – and maybe, who knows? Perhaps it *is* karma for wrongs in the past. But we're in the present, now. The present, you understand?' His voice became loud. 'And your Dalai Lama should *do* something. Instead, he sits on his arse, in his palace, king of Hollywood, king of the Himalayas . . .'

I felt the heat in his words, the anger beneath. 'Enough!' I said, in English, and then in Hindi, 'Bas!' I walked out of the room with the tray and the dirty plates and pushed hard through the swing doors. I was sweating. My face was hot. I wanted to hit the man with fists and words. To ask if he knew what it was to walk across mountains, to walk to a better life, to seek a blessing from His Holiness. To have risked everything for this. To suffer frostbite and attacks from wild animals. Attacks from red-cap soldiers. I was full of my family's story. I was full of the wrongs of the world. I threw a plate into the sink and it broke against the tap.

'Sonam!' Memsahib called my name. I was known by my birth name back then.

'Your boy is some kind of Buddhist?' I heard the Britisher laughing and joking.

'Of course,' said Memsahib. 'And one should respect . . .'

'A Buddhist with a temper,' Sahib cut in, also laughing. 'Too smart for his own good . . .'

I stood in the kitchen. My breath came heavy. I saw myself in the small good-luck mirror, the green-and-gold mirror of Memsahib. The mirror she put up to soften that corner, she said, to bring harmony and good fortune.

I looked hard at myself in that mirror. I did not like my reflection. I did not like what I saw.

A young man in a vest and khaki trousers. A
rucksack at his feet.

New Delhi, December 1990

ARKAY

It was in India I let it all drop. My life to that point, it all fell away. You read about it, how folk fall apart or find themselves – or lose themselves, more like – and you can't really believe it, until it happens to you.

At first it did my head in, the arrivals hall at the airport, the pressure of people and placards with names and everyone calling at once. I'd travelled all over by then, but nothing like this. I'd drunk the plane dry. Miniatures, the works. In the humidity of arrivals a hangover took hold. Pain inched through my skull. It was rare I ever got a hangover. But one in the air is worth two on the ground, so they say. And after the scramble for trolleys and the heat, after the long queue at the State Bank of India, I got a government taxi – a small manky car, and maybe it wasn't really a government taxi – but it was good just to be out of the terminal and heading into the city centre. Huge fat raindrops fell on the cracked windscreen and streaked the dust on the back window.

Then something happened: I looked out the window and everything seemed familiar. Couldn't explain it. How you go to a place and you know it. Some past life, maybe, if you believe that stuff. There were cows, and camels and trucks. There were few streetlights, no neon. Bright posters of Indira Gandhi and

Nehru. A few signs for Kingfisher Beer. Despite everything, happiness fired through me. The rain came heavy. Great sheets of rain. 'End of monsoon rain,' said the driver. 'A late monsoon, we are having.' As the rain hit, people lying on the ground and in market barrows stirred and covered themselves with blue plastic.

Rolling thunder and fork lightning as we got close to the colony, past some old burnt-out cars and buildings. The taxi slowed down. It was a big white house, that's all I remember. My mind was on higher things. Like the three wee bottles in my hand luggage.

I got up the next morning not quite as early as planned and met the family. There was a kind of shrill Raj voice calling for chai from one of the bedrooms – Old Mrs Singh – the grandmother, I figured out later. I met the man of the house at breakfast, Mr Singh, with his firm handshake that felt more like a challenge and his questions about what my father did. I didn't take to him at first and it was clear this was mutual. But his wife I liked, straight up. She was a little distracted, she said. She apologized for the house. Things were in turmoil, she said. The servants were very unreliable.

'We need new boys,' she told me. 'Boys from Nepal are best. But maybe . . .' She paused. 'Maybe there is something wrong with the kitchen . . .'

'The kitchen?'

'It has a bad angle, I think. I've put mirrors these past six years and we've had nothing but trouble. Since our last good boy left.' The *Hindustan Times* was open on the table and it caught her eye. She paused and bent down to look. 'Since he went there,' she said, shaking her head, pointing to the headline.

The page showed an article about the gas disaster in Bhopal. It was almost the sixth anniversary. I read how water had flooded the tank at the factory, and the deadly gas escaped over the city. The factory had been allowed to run down. The usual cost-cutting.

'But why did he go to Bhopal?' I asked.

'His family were there.'

'Oh . . .'

'And he was our best boy,' she said. 'So clever. So hard to replace.'

Then the small boy from the night before pushed through the doors from the kitchen with a pot of tea and a plate of fruit and an omelette and placed these down and I turned to say thank you, and the Sikh gave a tight smile and looked over at his wife, and I noticed when the boy came through with the rest of the breakfast that they kind of ignored him, didn't address him or look him in the eye. And I wondered if I'd made a mistake. Something cultural that I'd missed.

I stayed there for a week, enjoying the life, having a rest, waited on hand-and-foot. Some afternoons I joined the local boys playing cricket in the park. Opposite the park, in a side street, I saw the Dalit kids playing cricket with a broom handle and an empty plastic bottle. And when I'd leave the park and head for the booze shop, the wee hole-in-the-wall, I'd see them near the drains staring after me, their empty bottle gone.

After a few days I even came to like old man Singh. We'd sit together of an evening and I'd listen while he drank whisky and soda and blethered non-stop about the Punjab, the tea planta-tions, all of it. By the end of the week I knew all his stories but one night he surprised me, just as I was plotting my escape – a quick walk round the colony to the boozerie on the corner.

'A ghost?' I put my drink down.

'On more than one occasion,' he said, and his voice grew loud. That's one thing I noticed. When he told a story, he turned the volume up.

'Some men couldn't handle the isolation. It got to them. The Britishers.' He narrowed his eyes, tried to remember where I was from.

'Scotland,' I said.

'A Britisher.'

I let it pass. Took another sip. Eyed up his drinks cabinet.

'One night, I'd gone to sleep early, before midnight. My room was on the second floor of the bungalow, all wooden beams and creaking floors, you understand . . .'

He paused for effect. All Edgar Allan Poe now, all whisky-ed up, and I nodded, to show that I understood.

'And I felt the bed shaking, from below. And my first thought was "A damn tusker!" This used to happen – elephants in the gardens – and once a tusker came into the house. I walked downstairs and saw nothing, but the roof shook again and the beam under my bed, and then I saw him, a young man with fair hair, walk right through the front door. Without opening it, you understand?'

'Aye,' I said, motioning to the decanter, and he called the servant boy to come over and pour for me and he was all fired up because I was into his story.

'Next day I told my manservant, Mohinder. And he said: "George Lilley, Sahib. Ghost of George Lilley. Also, I am seeing him." And I then found out this fellow hanged himself, fifty years before, from the beam in the living room, right under my bed.'

'Jesus.'

'And that's not all.' He was in full flight now, even pouring his own drink, and I managed another for myself and he was off again.

Half an hour later he pushed back his chair, picked up a leather pillbox, for his arthritis he said, and before I could do anything put the stopper back on the decanter. 'That's more than enough for one night.'

Enough for him, maybe. After he went up to bed I was at the drinks cabinet again. The servant boy saw me, and I winked at him. Old Man Singh was harmless, I knew that. But it was clearly time to leave else I'd go nuts, listening to his stories and drinking him dry.

I said goodbye two days later and headed north. Folk said the mountains there were like Scotland. I thought that might be something to see. So I took a train from Delhi to Pathankot. At a stall outside the station I bought a dozen Kingfisher. It was five hours solid to Dharamsala. The bus shook and then broke down, but it all sped past: the cattle tethered to mud houses, the roofs of local slate, the men herding buffalo; the dry streams and rivers with big white boulders. It was late when we reached Upper Dharamsala. A taxi driver left me at a guest house owned by his family on a ridge overlooking the valley. It seemed more than I could afford but I wasn't feeling clear, and next morning, couldn't remember giving my passport details, had to check that I still *had* my passport. And what I mind from that first day was the sun on my limbs, drinking chai, looking out from the

balcony over the spruce trees, *nothing like fucking Scotland*. I
opened another beer. Later that evening I tried to drink myself
away with two Belgian students. Woke up in a minging hostel
in Macleod Gange costing a handful of rupees a night.

I woke again with my mouth dry and the inside of my head dry,
like my brain was scraped against my skull. I couldn't believe I
was here. I'd had a thing about India since I was a kid. I'd first
seen the Taj Mahal on telly sandbagged against attack; it was
during the Bangladesh war. It was so white and glowing and different and I wanted to be there, somewhere with sun and heat,
somewhere far away.

Now I was here. In India. Wanting to *be* different. Every
Westerner I met it was the same story – wanting to slip off the
old self, to become snake-new. You'd think it was the Sixties.
Maybe for the West it was always the Sixties in India. I thought
it was the last gasp of the Raj; this need to re-create yourself in
another culture simply because you could. The sheer fucking
luxury of it. It did my head in. All these thoughts, crowding, as
I sat out on the balcony of the guest house. On a rooftop
below, women hung out their washing. On another rooftop
three monkeys stared out over the valley; the mist so dense it
resembled the sea. I ordered a coffee, room service, and thought
about a wee something else. I'd clocked the miniatures lying on
the floor – what the? Whothef— bought? Then decided against
it. Had two Cobras just to keep things steady. After breakfast I
walked along a gravel path to a monastery. Namgyal Monastery,
that was the name. Prayer flags tattered from branches or wound

around tree trunks. In rooms off the courtyard, bells rang at
each turn of the huge prayer wheels, and there were flashes of
red and gold as I walked past. The sun was bright and my head
hurt.

I got to the main temple. Inside, two monks sat cross-legged
on cushions, books open on low tables in front of them, rock-
ing and chanting together. The younger monk had purple
marks on one side of his face. The older monk had his eyes shut.
They both looked up and smiled as I walked in. I saw the offerings piled up on the altars along with the butter lamps and
candles: packets of Nice and Treff cream biscuits, Nutrichoice
cream crackers, mounds of oranges, a tin of Verka pure ghee. I
thought of a classic Tartan contribution: oatcakes, shortbread,
can of Tennent's maybe. Just the thought of the Tennent's set me
off. I tried to focus on the riot of colour on the walls, the scenes
from the life of the Buddha. The sandalwood incense scenting
the room, how the calm lapped over me, how I could rest in
that calm for a minute, shut my eyes even, let myself sink into
it. But it seemed too easy and too difficult, and the next minute
I was out of there.

Back in Macleod Gange I drifted into a bookshop. On
impulse I bought two books by the Dalai Lama. I sat out on the
balcony overlooking the valley; a book open on my lap; a dozen
bottles under my chair.

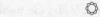

I got into a routine, started going down the monastery after
breakfast, to see the debates in the courtyard. The debaters were
monks from the School of Dialectics; some of them only boys.

The debates were loud and physical and fast-paced. I'd not seen anything like it before. The younger monks twisted and ducked, maroon robes flying, then swapped position. The older monks were less quick on their feet, more relaxed, less heated in their arguments. They clapped their palms, right hand over left, and there were cries of *Ha* to mark a point. It was pure magic.

One afternoon there was a dance performance, in aid of Tibetan orphans in the Childrens' Village. At the back of the stage, I saw a small bent man in ceremonial costume, stretching, rotating his hands and ankles. I recognized the old monk from Namgyal. He couldn't walk very well. He was an old man, no flesh on him, bow-legged, splay feet. But watching him dance this day was a revelation. When he danced he was a different person. Lit up from within. After the concert, as he edged out into the street, he saw me standing near the stage and motioned me over. 'England?' he asked.

I shook my head. 'Scotland.'

'Teach English?' The old monk smiled.

I smiled back, shook my head again. 'No.'

'Accha,' said the monk. 'Good.' And he laughed. It was a deep, happy sound. He clapped his hands together. 'Tomorrow, we start.'

I'd been looking to do something different, be someone different, what with every day the same: drinking and drifting with other tourists and the traveller chat. I was just bored with it. *How much? How far? How long?* The shite distinction between tourist and traveller. One night I couldn't take it any more. *We're*

all fucking tourists. This went down badly in the guest house. People always want to believe they're somehow different. It's understandable. I've wanted to believe it myself.

The next day, late morning, I walked down towards lower Dharamsala, my mouth dry and my mind kind of bruised. I'd been out with some French boys the night before, drank rum and beer, smoked lots of hash. Then back in my room, alone, the time I liked best, no pretence of social drinking. The Zen time. Just me and the bottles and the blank wall.

So I stood outside the old monk's room in the monastery feeling rough. I'd showered, combed my hair, brushed my teeth, freshened up. Put on a crumpled clean shirt with a collar; wanting to show some respect. Didn't really know why I was there, but it was something about him. So direct and in-the-moment. And I was flattered, to be honest, flattered that the old monk had singled me out, for whatever reason. There was the vague thought that I'd nothing to lose – fuck knows, might even learn something. Something more than traveller shite. This is the way my mind ran. I had an English-language text-book under one arm, bought second-hand for a few rupees. At the door, the old monk smiled, accepted the book, sat me down on a floor cushion and looked at me close – at my red eyes, the sweat beading my forehead. 'You have this problem,' he said, cutting straight to the chase. I shook my head. 'No problems,' I said. 'No more than average.' Tried to joke my way out but the monk was serious. And that was how it began. For the monk – Lama Shastri – dancing and meditation were his life. For years he trained in the early mornings with the bells and weights on the ankles and then again in the late afternoons. A ceremonial dancer. He knew English, he said, but it was the chat he was wanting. In return, he'd teach me meditation. It seemed a fair swap.

Dance, like meditation, like life, is in the training, not only the performance, Lama told me. Everyone wants to conquer anger and fear, he said. But no one ever asks to conquer desire. We're attached to these desires, identify with them. 'It's all attachment,' he said. 'Know this.' Then, quite out of the blue: 'The addict is a seeker. Accept this.' He paused, scanned my face. 'What are you seeking?'

I couldn't answer, caught out by the question, and started turning the pages of the textbook, angry all of a sudden. *What was he on about?*

'One day you will know,' said Lama. 'One day, we all know.'

We had a routine after that, and we never talked of the other stuff again. He didn't know the half of it, really – how hammered I used to get. But I always turned up for lessons, always on time, and it gave me a focus, a certain way with the tourists, especially the women. After lessons we'd walk the track between Macleod Gange and the monastery. Some days we sat under a pine tree, Lama on one side, me on the other. We'd sit like this for a time in silence and I learnt to focus on the breath. In spite of myself, I took to it. Could lose myself in it. Sometimes, big red monkeys circled near. Sometimes we sat so long it was like the tree became my spine, imprinted itself, then a question from Lama would shatter the calm, like a blow to the head: 'This morning, when washing your face, what did you learn?' At first I tensed up, unable to watch the breath, waiting

for the questions, feeling the anxiety rise and wanting a drink.
Then I learnt to relax because Lama gave me no choice.

He was always doing my head in.

'Why don't we remember our past lives?' I asked him one
day.

'Because it's too much burden,' he said. 'Too many memories. But previous lives shadow us. Our likings, our hatreds, the
people we meet, are clues to these pasts.'

'But what's the point of being reborn?' I asked Lama. 'What's
the point?'

Lama Shastri smiled. 'The Buddha said, the point was to
learn how to stop.'

I confessed to Lama: I've done stupid things. Almost killed a
man once, I said, thinking of my youth in the village. Then my
time in Australia. Istanbul. Greece. Though I tried to play it all
down, even to myself. Lama, serious and quiet for a moment,
closed his eyes: 'A man of violence who comes to a good end –
I will take him for my teacher.'

'The Buddha said that?'

He shook his head. 'No, it's from the Tao.'

He kept me on my toes.

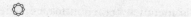

I watched the breath come and go. I watched it rise up my
spine. I learnt to meditate – who would've thought? And Lama
encouraged, drew it out of me, some kind of better – I want to

say 'self', but of course that's not it. My 'self' got a kicking. But for sure I got better with the self I was. With all the distractions of ego, as Lama would say. I became less thrown about. I'd sit with the breath and watch the thoughts. Over six months I started to drink a bit less in the evenings, less in the afternoons; even the mornings lost their edge. Sometimes in meditation I found I could sigh for Scotland. Involuntary sighs that took me by surprise; sighing for things long gone. Sighing for things I didn't even know I missed.

◇

One day I had a question for Lama. I asked him why, out of all the foreigners in Dharamsala, he'd chosen me. There were others better qualified. My ego wanted an answer.

'But you chose me!' he said.

I had to sit with that for a while. Let it sink in.

'I'm changing,' I said to Lama one day. 'I want to thank you.'

'You were ready for change.' He paused. 'No change if not ready.'

Shortly after this, the Dalai Lama returned to Dharamsala. For the Tibetans it was always a celebration: *His Holiness is coming.* Shopkeepers hung banners and placed butter lamps and offerings in their windows. The town was transformed. People dressed in their best clothes and lined the streets, hoping for a glimpse when the cavalcade of Mercedes went by.

I lined up with Lama and all the Tibetans and another monk called Naga we'd met some weeks before at the monastery debates. Naga had a belly and dark purple stains on one cheek. Ages with me, more or less; light on his feet, though he had a slight limp. He made his points rapid-fire, *Ha, Ha, Hahnji*? He always commanded a crowd. Lama introduced us and that's how I came to teach both of them. Naga knew far more about language than me, that's a fact. He took everything in. All the words I could throw at him. He'd taught himself young, listening to the foreigners on the slopes. He'd taught himself when he was a domestic in Delhi, learning from the books in the house. He was sharp as a tack. Smart as they come.

So the three of us stood there as the cars sped by and the Dalai Lama looked out the window, raised his hand and smiled. The Tibetans bowed their heads. Stood for some minutes, silent, looking after the car before returning to work. Then the laughing and joking began, a festive atmosphere, and I was enjoying myself. As the crowd broke up I heard a large American woman say in a loud, disappointed voice: 'That was it? Like, it's over now? That was it?' I looked over at Lama and Naga and they smiled and shrugged. I rolled my eyes, feeling superior in that moment. But a wee bit of knowledge is a dangerous thing.

A few days later, word spread about a public audience. I queued at Tibetan security and again at Indian security to get my passport checked. The following day I passed through two metal detectors and a body search to line up in the garden of the official house. The old folk and the sick were first in line. Everyone waited two hours in the hot sun and then suddenly he appeared on the verandah, smaller and more stooped than I imagined, flanked by bodyguards and monks. The queue snaked forward. Then it was my turn. He smiled, we grasped hands. Up close, the Dalai Lama had clear brown eyes and a direct gaze. I bowed my head. 'Thank you,' I said, not even sure why, but when I walked away my eyes were wet like everyone else and there was the feeling of something special, something beyond words. Monks gave out red threads, the knot blessed by the Big Man himself. People tied these threads around their wrists and necks. Up ahead of me was the American woman again, her voice insistent as we left the gardens: 'Is that all? I mean it was over sooo quick.' Another American turned to her, trying to control his impatience, and said: 'That's the whole point, lady. Impermanence, see. The importance of the moment.'

'Oh,' she said and there was hurt in her voice. 'OK. OK. Forgeddit.'

Later I sat on a step overlooking the valley, thinking about the day. I realised the American woman was right – it'd gone way too quick, that time with the Dalai Lama. The wait in the sunshine, the energy charge through the crowd, the Tibetan security calm yet alert, smiling in their suits. Who'd ever seen a security man smile? The maroon robes of the monks like a curtain either side of the Dalai Lama. I wanted to be back there. I seemed to remember it in close detail and I remembered it as perfect and myself in that moment as someone new. A flash of something. Wanting to prolong the moment because it was pure magic. I tried not to hold on, but I didn't want to lose it. The more conscious I was of the calm, the more I craved it. I touched the red thread at my wrist and sat for some time on the balcony of the guest house. I sat with the breath, tried to stay there with the still feeling – happiness, even – before it all started up again, the eternal hard clamour for the old comfort, drowning the silence, prising the cap off the bottle, tilting it back and down, the old ritual, trying to make the feeling last. I couldn't help myself, the old story, and in that instant, I understood the

American woman. I'd thought I was better, what with my meditation and my bit of reading and my pals in the monastery, but that was all ego. Creating a barrier. It hit me that there was no fucking difference between us.

It was then I made the decision. I could remain a spiritual tourist or commit to something. I would take Refuge, the Buddhist ceremony. I was on the path. Now I could go the whole hog.

The night before the ceremony, before vowing off the drink, I went on a bender with three young Israelis. It was the last time; I swore it'd be the last. Things'd be different now, I told myself. I'd be different. I matched them pint for pint and then some. They passed out long before I did, and I took the rest of the beer back to my own room. Next day I slept through the alarm clock and Naga and Lama had to chap at my door. They ran water in the bucket for a shower; they brought chai, exchanged worried looks. They came with me in the bus to the monastery. Alcohol steamed from my skin. All I wanted was another drink. I kept my head down; stayed silent on the three-hour trip. Shame-filled that on this day of all days I couldn't be sober and alert. Eventually I faced them. 'This is the last time,' I promised, 'it won't happen again.' In the temple, I repeated the three commitments to the Buddha, to the Dharma, to the Sangha. I knelt down unsteady, hands folded in namaste. The Lama cut hair from my crown and placed it in a small bowl. A young monk poured water from a spouted pitcher and my scalp tingled, the ache in my head temporarily soothed. I got my Dharma name in a small yellow book. I received a blessing. I repeated the vows. I felt happy and light, everything I could want to feel in that moment. I'm on my path, I told myself.

Everything was now behind me, I was sure of it, a new life stretching ahead.

How easy. To drop one life. To start another. I'd done it before.

After the ceremony, no big surprise. My mood leapt, soared. For a week I was high as a kite. And then, I fell back. Same old. 'But what did you expect?' Lama tried to comfort me. 'Big changes in one day?' I struggled, but I tried to be mindful, as they say. I tried to slow with the drink. But sometimes the feeling hit hard, a sense of not measuring up, and I'd sit there like a fool with the blank wall and the cushion and sob like a wean.

EARLY PRINTS

A young girl at the beach. She holds out her hand to the camera. There is a small round pebble in her palm and she squints against the light.

St Kilda Beach, Australia, 1966

FRANÇOISE

A humid summer day. The mercury tops one hundred degrees and across the city the skies hang heavy from bushfires in the Dandenongs. In the Royal Women's Hospital, after a fortnight of such temperatures, the air conditioning fails. The nurses put bed sheets in buckets of water then drape the wet sheets from the windows. A light breeze from pedestal fans lifts the cloth, cooling the new mothers and babies.

My mother grips the metal edge of the bed. Her feet are in leather stirrups; they slip and sweat in the heat. She opens her mouth; twists and grimaces; she can't push any more and flags her right hand in surrender.

The doctor slices across and I'm borne up in his long thin hands, the cord bloody, looped round my neck. 'A girl,' the doctor says as he disentangles the cord, something triumphant in the voice, the voice he always uses at a successful birth. He hands the baby to the nurse. 'Congratulations,' he says to my mother, patting her on the shoulder. The nurse washes me and then I'm placed on my mother's breast. My mother has trouble feeding.

Meanwhile my father sits out in the corridor along with all the other men waiting to be called. He's nervous. He's staring at the form guide thinking about the 3.15 at Caulfield, the smell of bleach around him, the flowers across his lap. Lemon calla lilies in plastic, the petals closed. The only flowers left at the service station. 'Funeral?' the petrol attendant asked, seeing the man in the suit and the choice of bouquet. My father emptied his pockets on the counter, scattering change. *Were the flowers all wrong? He knew shit about flowers.* He's sweating in his dark blue suit and white shirt, the top button open, the tie undone, and when the nurse brings a vase he's relieved there's no mention of funerals. Two of the lilies burst open, a pink blast as they hit the water. 'They're thirsty.' The nurse smiles. 'This heat.' She sighs, wiping the back of her palm across her damp forehead. He has a camera with him. A Polaroid. He asks the nurse to take a photo.

He wants to call me Françoise.

'A name like that. They'll think she's up herself.' My mother isn't happy.

'We'll shorten it to Fran.'

He'd once seen the name in a book, my father said. And more important, it was the name of a favourite horse. He'd always liked the sound of it.

Who knows if that's the way it happened? I piece it together, the colours and the sounds of it, this early life when I still had two parents. I fix it in memory. I frame it like that.

My father was the local postman and a well-known gambler. He rose early for his bicycle round through the neighbourhood. He knew all the early risers; he knew every barking dog; would wave to the milkman coming back. He enjoyed his job and people enjoyed him; there were bottles of beer left out for him at Christmas, sometimes even at Easter. My father was charming and good-looking, so people tell me, and there are photographs to prove it. My mother always loved him in that painful way, that swings-and-roundabouts kind of way. We lived well at times when he was winning, when he got lucky. At other times we hung on, when there was barely enough for the mortgage or to buy milk.

I have memories of a big warm shape holding me, reading to me, but I can't be sure that this is him. He died when I was young – a sudden heart attack in the street. He didn't leave a will, and there was no money when he died. My mother sold the house to pay for the debts and the funeral. We moved into a rented house and my mother went back to nursing, worked all sorts of shifts, and kept us both going. 'We'll make do,' she said.

I still have dreams about my father. The shape of his presence and absence. We're in a crowd of people. A throng pushing through a huge building, a garden courtyard, rows of archways, diamond sounds. There are so many people. At some point, we lose sight of each other and in the dream I'm an adult woman, not a child. I try to push back through the crowd, but it's a child's voice which carries through: *I've lost him*, I say to anyone who'll listen. *Has anyone seen my father?*

As an adult, you face loss, sooner or later. But as a child it means something different.

After his death, I dreamt of being somewhere else. I dreamt

of a block of stone which could change shape – now a bird; now a boat; now an aeroplane. A magic stone which would take me nightly to somewhere new. I went looking for this stone one day when the tide was out and the wind lightly pleated the sea. My mother and I walked for hours along the small beach at St Kilda – sometimes she could indulge me – trying to find the right dreaming stone. A smooth, flat, dark stone, I insisted, and we walked until I found it. I kept that stone for years, placed the stone outside my bedroom window, focused my nights upon it. Now it sits on a shelf outside my darkroom.

When I was small I'd take a block of soap and a knife and spend an afternoon carving the soap into different shapes. I'd find pieces of branch and wood and bend and carve them for hours. I'd begin again and again until I was happy with what I'd done. I'd model plasticine into animals and human figures and the pyramids of Egypt I'd seen on our black-and-white television. I'd make origami patterns with paper and cardboard. I was always taking one thing and making something else. I'd place these objects against a window and watch the way the light changed as it hit, and the shadows called up.

For as long as I can remember I've heard colours and seen sounds. A summer sky still glockenspiels behind my eyes. As a child I'd look up through the car windscreen on a hot afternoon: 'The sun is whistling,' I'd say. 'My head hurts.'

With black-and-white it's the gradations and tonings that I love. All the shaded joys and sadness. The extremes played off against each other. It's more difficult in black-and-white to make a good image. And I've always been drawn towards the difficult. Of course I could make a fortune with acid sunsets and furry cats, green mountains and clear blue lakes. Colour sells, so I'm told. And cats. But not everyone has it in them to be an entertainer.

My mother, early on: 'Your senses are all jumbled.' She'd frown when I'd call any matt surface blue or hear a child's cry as purple. 'You imagine things,' my mother would say.

At the beach on summer holidays I'd make sandcastles. Flowing forms – archways and tunnels and waves of sand. Packing the sand and tamping it down. I'd spend hours at it. Turn around to display my handiwork. Ask my mother to take a photograph. My mother would adjust her sunglasses, pull the brim of her sunhat down. 'That's not a sandcastle,' my mother would say, in a disturbed, slow tone. 'Look at what the other children are doing. That's not a sandcastle.'

'It's *my* sandcastle,' I'd say. 'It's *mine*.' Even at that age – I could've been no more than five or six – resisting her. I'd pick up my father's old Polaroid and take the photo myself.

And always at the end of the holiday, never wanting to return. Never wanting to go back to where I'd started, back to the monotone house. To ordinary life where the colours were so loud and I was all wrong.

'There's something not right,' my mother told the doctor. 'Something out of whack.' After the tests he said, 'There's nothing to worry about. Nothing at all. It's what we call synaesthesia.' Being a good Catholic, he added, 'You could say she's lucky. You could even say she's blessed.'

When he explained all this my mother said: 'Oh no. Don't tell me. I've got enough on my plate. Don't tell me she's special.'

From a young age I could smell the passage of time, but I kept that to myself.

○

My father died and my mother clung to his memory. She always spoke as if he'd died only the day before. For years she refused to part with his belongings. His suits still hung in the wardrobe along with his blue postal shirts, cleaned and ironed. There were drawers full of yellowing copies of the form guide and old betting slips. She still jolted upright at the ring of the telephone, believing it could only bring bad news. I remember little of my father's funeral but I clearly remember the bottles of Valium in the bathroom cupboard. For her nerves, she said. I was given half a Valium with milk before my first Holy Confession. I remember my mother's anxiety and then the blank calm face. All the mothers then had blank calm faces.

I was over-sensitive, that's what my mother said. I used to cry a lot for no apparent reason. There was a tree in the front yard and I used to hide high up in the branches. My mother never came looking and I wanted so much to be found. I carved shapes into the branches with a kitchen knife, counted the sounds of the leaves. At Mass I could see the Virgin singing. It was a blue sound in the candle flames and I prayed to her but she never seemed to answer.

After my father's death Grandpa came to live with us and I loved him, my father's father. He was kind and funny and it was Grandpa who really encouraged me to draw. He taught me how to really *see*. I had trouble with reading and writing. But he would read to me and encourage me to make things. 'She's got something,' he'd say to my mother and to anyone else who'd listen. 'She's got an eye.'

'I don't know what she's got,' my mother would say. 'I don't know who she takes after.' I'd come home with drawings and gold stars from the teacher. I'd come home with sculptures made from sardine tins and bits of soap. I'd offer them up to her. She'd examine them and then turn away from me, saying: 'Don't get too big for your boots, Fran. Mind now. There's always someone better round the corner.'

'Come and show me,' Grandpa would say, frowning at my mother, stretching out his hand, peering at my work over his half-glasses. 'That's a beauty.'

'Don't spoil her,' she'd sigh, lighting up another cigarette, inhaling and exhaling deeply. 'She'll get tickets on herself.'

For my birthday that year, Grandpa bought me a camera. A Polaroid. My first real camera.

I'm eight years old and sent home with a note from Mrs Irvine, our teacher. 'Give this to your mummy,' she says, pressing the note into my palm, watching me to make sure I put it in my schoolbag.

At home, I remember the note. My mother taps her foot and sighs as she reads it. She has a sigh for every occasion. Sometimes the house is so full of her sighs it makes me want to run.

When I hear her sigh this time I'm tempted, but I know it's no use, that you can only ever run a little way away. My mother crumples the note in her apron pocket and moves to the stove to put the kettle on, scraping in that same pocket for matches and in the cupboard above the sink for her cigarettes. My eyes follow her, tracking her movements like a satellite, and I wait, knowing I've done something wrong.

'It's the crying,' she says, sitting down and striking a match. 'The school's worried. God only knows what they think. What kind of a mother?'

She kneels down in front of me, blowing smoke through her nose, and puts her arms on my shoulders, tilts my chin up. 'I try my best, Fran. It's not easy, God knows. But I try my best.'

I know this and I put up my arms and hug her for a sweet short time, wanting to make her feel better. She pulls away from me and says: 'They want you to see someone, a doctor; he'll help you. You'll do that for me, won't you Fran? You'll go see him?'

'Yes,' I say. Because I'd do anything for her, anything to make her happy. Because she's my mother. The only one I have.

On a clear winter morning I'm sitting on a cushion, buckled into the front seat, feeling like a grown-up, and my mother is driving the old EH Holden to a suburb I've never seen before, where the houses are big and the gardens even bigger and most have built-in swimming pools.

'The houses here.' My mother sniffs and sighs a muddy sigh. 'Full of New Australians. Such big houses.'

We pull up outside a brick house painted white with a dark trim around the windows. I can see a little of it above the hedge. I'm full of the newness of it all. No one in our street has hedges or brick houses, all the houses are weatherboard. We open a wrought-iron gate and walk down a path edged with rose bushes. It looks like a gingerbread house, like something from England, and I tell my mother this and she says, 'Thank God the school is paying. I hope you'll be a good girl. I hope you'll be grateful.'

'I will,' I say.

There's a man-dark shape behind the glass panel in the door. When he opens the door, the stained glass scatters colour, makes percussion sounds across the carpet. He's a big man in a woollen sports coat and he's got dark hair and dark eyes. 'His name is Dr Pizarro,' says my mother. 'Be good for him.' He bends down to shake my hand like a grown-up, and then he shakes my mother's hand, and tells her not to worry. His voice is kind and he smells of aftershave. My mother says goodbye and that she'll be back in an hour, she's got shopping to do. I feel a cool panic as I see her go, but I take the man's hand and he guides me down the long hallway with the thick quiet carpet and into a side room with the blinds half-drawn and low lamps in the corner, even though it's sunny outside, and he draws up a leather armchair and directs me to a seat on the other side of his desk, a kid's-size seat with cushions. On the desk there's paper and crayons and plasticine. There's a fire in the grate, a real fire, not a gas one, and the room is warm and cosy and I want to sink back in my cushions and push the crayons around the paper and close my eyes, but before I can do this he asks me to draw my house with all the people in it and then he asks me about the people and the colours I've used and why my father is up there on the roof, with wings.

He gets out a big leather book and opens each page and all I have to do is look at the black-and-white pictures. He calls them inkblots and asks me to describe what I see. I hear red and I tell him. I'm loving this game, really loving it, and I tell him all the colours and the sounds and then I start up with the stories and he sits back and listens, he doesn't try to stop me or tell me I'm exaggerating. I tell him that one of the shapes is a baby kangaroo.

'A girl joey or a boy?'

'A boy,' I say. And I tell him the story of this joey who has lost his mother and his father, who is an orphan, and all too soon the doorbell goes and we walk down the thick carpet and the house is very still and I wonder if the doctor-man has a wife or children and if they swim in the pool every day and then my mother is at the door and the first thing she says is, 'I hope you've been good for Dr Pizarro.' He laughs and says, 'More than good.' And this makes me happy because I know it's true and we smile at each other and I wave to him as I take my mother's hand and he says, 'See you next Saturday.' I'm so happy I forget to cry for a week.

In the evening when my mother and grandfather sit around the Formica table and discuss the day, him over a beer, my mother with a shandy, I hear her say: 'Crayons and kangaroos?'

'Seemed to do the trick,' said Grandpa.

Every Saturday morning for I don't know how long, we drive to Dr Pizarro's and I run down the garden path to meet him. I can't wait to get to the inkblots – by now I'm making my own inkblots at home and telling him what I hear there – and my continuing story of the kangaroos and the green thump of their tails. A good story, he says, sad and funny, like all good stories should be. I don't remember him talking very much at all, just that the hour would go quickly, too quickly. I'd made a plasticine model of the baby joey who was an orphan, but no longer cried because he'd learnt to draw with his tail in the sand.

I took a Polaroid of the joey with me. The day came when the Doctor closed the inkblot book, our last day, and I cried long and hard at the thought of leaving this room, the first I'd cried in all the time I'd been going there, but my mother said: 'The Doctor says you're better, no more tears now. Thank the Doctor.' I thanked him and he hugged me and I hugged him back and on the way home my mother stopped and bought me a vanilla milkshake and that evening when I got out of bed and stood in the hallway behind the kitchen door listening to the adult conversation, I heard my mother pour a beer for my grandfather and sigh a purple sigh: 'She loved that shrink more than me.'

'He's been good for her.'

'We'll see.'

Years after when I asked her about my Saturday mornings with Dr Pizarro, tried to talk about why I was sent there in the first place, she said: 'You were highly strung. It's so long ago, who knows why?' She looked over at me, tapped her fingers on the table. 'But maybe. Maybe you think it was my fault?'

'No,' I said, uncertain. The older I got the more uncertain I was around her.

'He stopped the waterworks,' she said. 'Thank God for that.' She lit another cigarette and inhaled. 'Too highly strung,' she repeated.

A small boy in a striped football scarf plays in the snow.

West Lothian, Scotland, 1966

ARKAY

At seventeen I could drink twenty pints and still go for a run the next morning. This is what it meant in the village to be a man. But I got away from the village, and in India I gave up the drink. But in truth, it was waiting for me all along. All those years, waiting for me to slip up. Waiting to draw me back. *Drink, my wee pal.*

There was an old man in the village, old Eddie, always stumbling out of the Central at closing. Hurling himself on the pavement. One night, I saw Eddie standing in the middle of the street, cursing a half-empty bottle of whisky, tears down his face. 'I never want tae see ye again,' he cursed and raged at the bottle as if it were a person. 'Mind? Never again.'

But of course, Eddie. Everyone said, *couldnae keep away.*

On the wagon or off the wagon. What did it matter? There was the fact of the wagon, the direction it was going, where it could take you. The drink lit you up from inside, made you feel special, made you feel good. Couldn't last. Next morning, made you feel shite, turned everything dark. Wait for the wheel to turn, the next drink, take you back to the good, the flame inside.

Drink, my wee pal.

☼

I'm a young boy, fourteen years old, fighting in the street. There's a circle of men and a Celtic football scarf. There's a broken bottle. Cuts on my face and my nose is broken. I'm lying in a red pool, the scarf at my feet and nearby, the graffiti: *papist scum*. I drag myself home, leaving pink trails in the snow. It's almost Christmas. I fall down at the front door. My mother and father pull me inside. 'What happened to ye?' They're shouting at me from a long way off. 'Was it the football?'

'Aye,' I'm saying. 'But more than the football.'

My father nods and pulls me to my feet. 'Nae bother.' Looks down at me with a tight smile of satisfaction. We both know it's a rite of passage, how it happens like this in the village.

Their voices are muffled. The left side of my head is under-water. I swallow and can't hear myself do it. It's my left eardrum. I yawn and tap the left side of my head with my hand and still no sound. Silence hits me from the left and at my back, silence.

We lived in an old shale-mining village between Edinburgh and Glasgow. It was all Catholics in our scheme, known locally as the Vatican. Green among the Orange. I spent my youth fighting. Developed a taste for it. Developed a taste for the drink – that fierce combination. Almost killed a man once. An Orangeman, after an Old Firm game. A good kicking I gave him, then I was away. Left the man bleeding and drunk. The man was concussed but he recovered. They said he was never the same after that, never the same. Maybe it was an exaggera-tion. There was plenty of that in the village. I got a name as a hard man, a bit of a nutter, but it was all a mistake, didn't know my own, blamed it on the drink; a million excuses. And I wasn't interested in a reputation.

I left the village as soon as I could, ran from the drink and the fighting. Kept running.

✿

Australia. As far away as I could get. Emigrated at seventeen; found work picking fruit. Oranges and grapes up near the New South Wales border. We slept in heat-blazed caravans. Nights spent in a pub with the longest bar in the southern hemisphere. Followed the seasonal workers and drifters up the East Coast, brawling and drinking. Met a girl and got her pregnant. Married her for the passport. And there I was at twenty, a married man. I knew I didn't love her. And although it hurt, hurt her more than it did me, it was pure relief when she lost the baby. This happened early on. By then I was in debt *up to my back teeth*, as she kept saying. We moved to Melbourne because moving was always better than staying. One day I packed the green Ford with all our stuff, which wasn't much, drove to the Flemington racetrack, put my wife in the driver's seat, told her to stay there, then strode into the ground as if my life was about to change. Worked my way around the crowd, tapped the Scots and the Irish expats, sold tickets in a charity that didn't exist. I remembered the scams from the village. Worked the crowd, went outside, jumped behind the wheel and drove to Queensland with three hundred dollars in my pocket. I whistled in the heat and the long stretches of road. Whistled all the way there.

A year later up north, tried the same scam. Walked cool as a cucumber from the racetrack, bottle of Bundy in hand, two hundred dollars in my pocket, wife behind the wheel; her nephews in the back seat, heat pressing through the windscreen. Saw them sitting there waiting for me as I came out the gate and crossed the car park. I paused for a moment, took the cap off the bottle. Kept walking. Never looked back.

❁

I signed on as a kitchen hand with a cargo ship. We sailed all over the Med and it wasn't a bad life, truth be told. You could be whoever, no questions asked. For most of that time I kept my head down. Worked solid. Kept out of trouble. Of course something had to give.

It happened in Istanbul. We sailed up the Bosphorus just as it was getting dark. Had a couple hours off and I wandered down Yerebatan, listening to the sound of gulls and stray dogs, watching the pigeons free-fall round the minarets. Then back through Eminonu to the ferry terminus. I heard footsteps behind me, and a young man was at my side, a hand at my elbow, asking me for a light. We fell into easy conversation. He introduced himself in English with an American accent: *Wolfgang*, a student from Munich, son of a German father and Turkish mother. He was on vacation, he said, working part-time on the family stall at the spice bazaar. Had I been to the spice bazaar? He also worked in his vacations as a *reiseführer*, because his German was good and his English even better. 'And what do you think of my English? A tour guide with good German and good English is indispensable, nicht wahr?' He kind of drew me in. Open-faced. Sincere. Caught me off guard. 'If you want anything, I have contacts,' Wolfgang continued, a hand on my shoulder. His voice lowered. 'Women,' he said. 'You want women?' It'd been a while and I hardened at the thought and then, just as quick, the desire left me. I remembered the women I'd seen around the ports. Always skelf-thin and empty-eyed, scabs on their forearms. I shook my head. 'Boys?' Wolfgang persisted. 'Boys, you want boys?' No, I said, shaking my head. I was clear on that score. Wolfgang looked at me closely, assessing my needs. 'Hashish? Opium, maybe?' I looked at a point over my shoulder, not to seem too keen. 'Maybe,' I said. I followed him to the spice bazaar through the colours and the scents. It was near closing-time and the customers had thinned out. I followed him to a stall at the back of the bazaar and saw three heavy men with dour faces sat behind pyramids of saffron and cloves. There was something about the set of their shoulders and the cramped space. Something was off. *Whatthefu?* Looking over, I saw that I'd been played at my own game, my old game, and that I couldn't take them on. I had to think fast, think on my feet. I stopped and turned to Wolfgang, holding my belly. 'I'm not feeling so good.' Wolfgang looked at the three men waiting at the end of the bazaar and with a slight shrug directed me to the urinal block. We walked back the way we'd come. Wolfgang said he'd meet me again at the entrance and that was his first big mistake. *Don't let the mark out of your sight, that's the first rule.* The boy was more of an amateur than he seemed and as soon as he turned to light another cigarette, I looped past the minging toilets and disappeared into the crowd.

To steady myself I went for a drink, and then another. I knew I had to get back to the ship, but I started raging against the boy, Wolfgang, trying to take me for a ride. An hour later I went looking for him outside the spice bazaar, and in an empty-crate laneway I found him. It was silent and quick and I left him bleeding in the gutter like a sacrificial goat. I was pleased in that minute, but the feeling didn't last. The adrenaline wore off and I drifted to a club full of Westerners. I sat at the bar all night, morose, drinking beer and vodka shooters, watching Turkish men in shoulder pads moonwalk across the floor. I moved on to halves, but felt sober as a judge. Sometimes it was like that. Sometimes the feelings just couldn't be drunk down.

I jumped ship. I had to get out of Istanbul.

I got a map, closed my eyes, pointed to the map. I had my finger on a place and I went there. It was that simple. Got a bus and arrived the next day at the small town of Didim. Found a dirty *pension* and woke the next day raw-headed, the usual, looking out over broken columns and pillars and the snake-curled head of a Medusa in stone. 'One of the last great Hellenic sites', the *pension* man said. After strong coffee – couldn't face the breakfast, all cheeses and meats – I wandered round the site and it was then I met Irfan. He was struggling up the hill with what looked like a block of marble in a wheelbarrow. 'Not marble,' he said, glad to stop beside the wall and rest. 'Onyx.' Irfan invited me to his shop. 'Stay,' he said. 'See how I work.' I met his cousin, who proclaimed Irfan the finest onyx carver in all Turkey. I watched him work in the small shed attached to the onyx shop. Irfan explained the differences in the stone – the white onyx, the green onyx and the black. Over the next two months I fell into a routine of visiting Irfan and his family after breakfast to drink tea, to talk, to help out in the shop. I was happy being a part of it all. A family. In the evenings we drank beer and raki, lots of raki. Then I'd take more bottles back to my room; sit drinking alone, the favourite time, drinking until I couldn't drink any more. One morning, Irfan dropped by the *pension*, saw me rinsing sheets in the grimy tub and smelt the strong urine smell. I gave some excuse – about the laundry, the lack of facilities – to cover my tracks.

I was always good at covering my tracks.

I enjoyed watching Irfan at his lathe crafting a vase as his father and his grandfather had taught him. I watched Irfan play with his children, watched him tender with his wife in her blue headscarf and missing front tooth, saw how indulgent he was with all of them and how they loved him. I watched Irfan cooking meat over the grill, throwing handfuls of salt and paprika over the meat. Standing there with a glass of raki in his hand until the meat was charcoaled and he was sweating with the effort of it, enough meat for an army, enough raki for twenty guests. More than enough. Irfan threw out his arms wide: 'I am a happy man. A lucky man. Inshallah!'

Everything he did – cooking, loving, talking, holding an onyx bowl in his great palm – he did with total love and absorption. Irfan had rarely travelled outside Didim, was happy with his family, his friends, his life. He'd distilled it all down, was happy with what God put in his way. He wasn't pulled by desires or ambitions other than to do his work well, to sell his beautiful onyx, to enjoy his wife and two daughters. He worked hard and lived simply. I envied him, that's the truth of it, hoping that if I stayed long enough some of that contentment with life, some of that ease, might rub off.

I stayed for eight weeks. Would've stayed longer but one day as I sat watching Irfan work, watching him shape the stone, things shifted. As I sat watching chess pieces emerge through his fingers, the bell went and a tourist walked in. 'Can you talk to him?' Irfan said, barely looking up from his lathe. I parted the curtain from the workshop into the showroom and saw the German standing there twisting his wedding ring. This is a test, I thought. I felt transparent. But money was running low and I swithered. The man looked at me and the decision was made. I'd always drawn a certain kind of man, always had, since back in the village. Now that I was older I knew how to play them. Payback. That was the cold hard fact of it and I played the German for a week, escorted him to the sites, then up to the hamam, arranged the boys and took the photographs. I played him right down. At the end of the week, after the wealthy German had gone and I'd trousered most of his money, I dropped by Irfan's workshop. He was there sitting on a stool looking out the window, resigned, expectant almost.

'Waiting for someone?'

'You,' Irfan said. Turning on the stool to look at me. 'I'm waiting for you to say goodbye.'

I smarted at the truth of it and wanted to put up an argument, but Irfan interrupted. 'You want to ask me, how do I know? It's the same, how I always know these things, I have some instinct.' He inhaled his cheap sharp cigarette. 'I wish it was not, but I always know what is about to happen.'

I was caught out. The decision made before I knew it fully myself, before I'd even thought it through. I realized I couldn't stay. I stood there and no words came, and then I gave in. 'Maybe it's true. That I was coming to say goodbye. To thank you. It's been magic,' I said. 'You, your family, I've learnt so much . . .'

'Not so much that you can stay?'

'No.' I was adamant now, there was no going back. In a minute, this is how it happens.

'You think your life can go on like this?' said Irfan. 'You could be a good person. Come back one day and show me what a good person you did become.'

I looked out the window along the dusty street. I could see a bus coming, whorls and patterns of dust. The bus would wait for thirty minutes before going on. There was my rucksack, my few belongings. How easy it would be, to walk out of my life here and never come back, my pockets full of deutschmarks. I had four rolls of film to develop. I had the addresses in Berlin. Suddenly I felt hard and clear. First I'd send a photograph to the German's work, and then, if needed, send it direct to the German's wife. There'd be a certain sum of money, I was sure of it. This could keep me going for some time, I thought. No harm in it. Worth a try. Maybe get me through Greece. Finance my travels.

I turned to Irfan. 'You set me up. To test me.'

'No.' Irfan was on his feet, shaking his head, gesturing at me with his cigarette. 'You, my friend, set yourself up.'

I shifted my weight from one foot to another. 'One day, you'll see. Everything you taught me, it wasn't for nothing.'

Then I went to my room at the *pension*, threw my clothes in the rucksack and ran for the bus.

Irfan was the first Bodhisattva of my life. Only later would it become clear to me. There were others, but he was the first. But I never did get back to Didim. Never got to show him the person I became.

A group of Westerners. Two porters squat in front with luggage on their backs, plastic bags around their feet.

Annapurna Mountains, Nepal, 1980

NAGA

1961. The midwife travelled with us on the long, long escape. We camped in caves, trekked through snow valleys, over mountain passes. After one month there was little tsampa or butter left and my mother made stew from the yak-skin bags. She soaked the leather until it swelled, cut it into small pieces, stewed it for hours until it looked like meat. There was no water left. We wet our lips with hoar-frost, we sheltered in hollow trees. We believed that the worst was behind us, that these obstacles were the path. That these difficulties were our guides, our teachers. Soon we would see His Holiness for our blessing. Soon we would be free.

We followed the Brahmaputra River. Many times we lost our way. Some of our party died, some were captured. There was always the fear of wild animals, of the cold, of the sound of rifle shots, of the red-cap soldiers. Finally we came to a junction of two rivers. We saw footprints; everything seemed strange, the warm air and the scent of unfamiliar trees. The ground turned rough, the mountains steeper, the way even more difficult as it always is at the end of a long journey when you do not know you are reaching the end. We passed over log bridges, the trees like a thick jungle, constant rain and mist. The trees grew taller. There were banana trees that we had never before seen. We did not know what the fruits were; we did not know to eat them. Many villagers helped us, brought us food – small rice cakes cooked in oil. We ate corn which made our bellies swell. There was no leather left. Soon, we said. Soon we will arrive. We lost sight of the Brahmaputra. We walked along the mountains above it. Then we saw it. The next pass was the border place. There was a noticeboard: *India*, it said, in English. *Bharat*, in coloured Hindi script. Still we could not believe. The guards called out 'Welcome' as we stumbled towards them. 'Welcome!' they called, in unfamiliar words. At the border of Tibet and India my mother's waters broke. It was a blue Himalayan day and the border men helped us. The midwife gave my mother munacka to chew, to ease the pain. I was born in an Indian Army truck, the cord around my neck; the midwife knifed through it. At the hostel my mother ate poppy seeds and almonds in milk. They fed her curd and ghee. They gave her tulsi boiled with cloves for her fever.

And I survived. The first of my mother's children to do so.

Some time after the blessing from His Holiness, after Dharamsala, we settled in the lowlands of Nepal. The family moved around, collected fuel wood, gathered herbs, collected pine resin. My father worked as a labourer, removing chaff from the wheat and rice by hand. All the labourers had infected eyes from pieces of chaff. Some went blind. While I was still young I left the forest in search of work. I went high up into the mountains to Annapurna and found a job as a porter. Then my family moved south, back to India, to the capital of Madhya

Pradesh. There was a new factory and many jobs there, my
father's brother wrote, many jobs. Leave the farm and come, he
urged. The factory made medicine for plants, he said. Pesticides.
It was a good job. My father and mother went, taking my small
sister with them.

On Annapurna the days were heavy with foreigners who
dreamt of the slopes. Early each morning I'd sit and watch these
people in their meditations and yoga salutes to the sun. I'd hear
their calls for chai – shrill, strange voices that hurt my ears. They
called me Sherpa. Many times I told them: 'Not Sherpa. My
family is from Tibet.'

It was the early days of the slopes, still new for the West. No
foreigner ever asked how we carried loads up the same clefts and
punishments of the mountains they did, but without the equipment. No foreigner ever asked if we were hungry or cold or too
thin. These people went back to tables of food and wine and
told stories of the terror and beauty and triumph – how they'd
been tested, every muscle and fibre, how their lungs gave out at
a certain altitude. How the porters were *incredible* – scaling peaks
like mountain goats. 'It's in the blood,' they would say.

When I became a monk, teaching meditation to Westerners,
I heard these stories. I'd turn to these well-meaning foreigners
and correct them as gently as I could: 'No. It's not in our blood.
Some of us come from the lowlands; our blood must thicken
when we climb up to look for work. We have one day only
before the tour groups come. We strap their bags to our fore-
heads and if we flag, if we fall ill or fall down, we are lost and
our families are lost.'

I remember the first time I said this. I looked at the pink faces
glowing round the full table. I felt for them, for their misplaced

earnestness. There was some anger in my voice, I admit. 'You climb and we die, sometimes it's that simple.' There was one man with a small beard, an academic, an expert on Nepal. 'But this tourism – it's a lifeline for you.' He said this very slowly, stressing the syllables for my benefit. 'Without it, many of your people would starve.'

'Yes,' I said in a calm voice. 'And for the West – someone else always carries the load.'

The academic, the expert on Nepal, turned away from me then. Words stuck on his fork.

There were the deaths of fellow porters. First it was my friend Shyam who was lost to the mountains. It happened on the lower slopes of Annapurna, in the early days. Our boss was a hard man and on that trip all porters took double loads just to earn enough. We slept in caves with one blanket between us. We stopped when Shyam fell ill. He began to vomit and his head hurt. We carried him down the slopes in a wicker basket slung between bamboo poles, plastic bags to cover our bodies against the cold. Our feet in sandshoes, sliding through the snow. Ice-winds bit our faces. Our friend never recovered.

After Shyam's death I packed my bag of salt and mustard oil. I packed kerosene for the lamp. I packed the plastic bags and sandshoes and again presented myself for work.

My body carries this past. The purple marks on my face from the teeth of cold winds. The body remembers. Every time I see pink eager faces leaning towards me, wanting to know the way out of samsara – this cycle of suffering – I long to show them my missing toes lost to frostbite, and the weft between that still bleeds when I walk. I long to show them my shoes packed with cotton, to ease the pain.

I want to tell them: 'Carry a load that's not yours for a day. Meditate on that.'

This, of course, would not be mindful. They would feel guilty. Westerners always have guilt. It's my karma to work with these spiritual tourists, to find compassion. To find our common heart.

My birth name is Sonam. Nagarjuna is my ordination name. My teacher said it was a name pointing in the right direction, away from the fire inside.

I shorten my ordination name because even after all these years I have yet to fill it. I struggle. Sometimes I suffer bad headaches. Even recently, my vision is blurred. 'This is your anger,' says our Tibetan doctor. 'You must curb this anger.' As a young man I was tested on the mountains. And when I look back at all my lives, I see I have been tested. Anger flares still if I allow it – an imprint from those times.

The year I turned twenty was the year I stopped work on the slopes. I'd been high up when my lungs filled and the headaches began. I thought I might not survive. It happened quickly and I began to hallucinate for my family. Sometimes I get a feeling of what is about to happen, but it's only when we look back that we can make patterns. Can see things more clearly. A friend, a fellow porter, saved me, eased me down the mountain, eased me out of the sickness. When I recovered, my friend said: 'Come to Delhi. Much work for boys from Nepal.' In Delhi, I met a small Nepalese man with two bodyguards and five rifles under his charpoy. The man offered to help me. I paid him a commission and two days later he left me at the gate of a large white house. He rang the bell and the Memsahib appeared at the door. My new life had begun.

☼

The Memsahib unlocked the door to the barsati roof. Showed me where to sleep and where to wash. Showed me where to hang clothes and how to fold and bundle them for the press-walli. Then to the kitchen. For lunch there was lentil roti, dhal with six different veg, curd, mung bean with lime pickle, followed by kulfi and gulab jamun. Memsahib showed me how to make these foods. While I was cooking, the Sardar came in. He spoke in Hindi. 'No tomatoes?'

The Memsahib sighed. 'No tomatoes.'

'Good.' He turned to me, as if noticing me for the first time. 'My wife is trying to kill me. A simple ask – no tomatoes – and what is served? Or I say – no sweets! And then kulfi, burfi, gulab jamun – what to do?'

'I'm not trying to kill you, Surjit. I'm trying to help you, only.'

He walked out of the kitchen and Memsahib said, 'Sahib's arthritis. Always he changes the diet. One day this, next day that, I can't keep up!'

At lunch, the Sardar and the Old Memsahib, his mother, sat stiff, without words. Then I brought through the food with Bisu, the other boy. The Sardar picked up a chapatti, looked down at his plate, then over at his wife.

'Take it back,' he said. 'Today, I need simple foods only. An omelette. Toast.'

I stood for a minute, not believing. I raised my eyebrows and the Sardar saw me.

'What's wrong, boy? Get to work.'

I pushed back into the kitchen and the swing door slammed.

'Is he simple, or simply insolent?' said the Sardar.

'He's new,' said Memsahib.

At the end of my second week a journalist and photographer came for the Old Memsahib. They wanted to interview her about the Gymkhana club – her favourite place for *luncheon*, she told me in her loud, clipped voice. Ever since she first came to Delhi it had been her favourite place. These people were doing a story, she said. They wanted to know some history from the time of the Raj.

I led them to her room, and she sat there in an antique lace sari – her mother's sari, she said – layers of pearls and diamonds at her neck. She put the final touches to her lipstick. I lifted the wooden blinds to let more light into the room, but she put up her hand. 'It's too harsh,' she said. 'It's not kind.'

I put down a tray of chai for the guests.

She posed easily for the camera. 'Always, they wanted my photograph,' she said, 'when the Britishers were here.'

'What was it like, back then?' the journalist asked as the photographer moved around. 'With the British?'

Old Memsahib leant forward, lowered her voice and her eyes and brought up her hands. 'It was all very wonderful!'

The photographer asked her to turn towards the light.

She part-angled her face. 'But I've endured a lot,' she continued. 'To be on top, as we were then, to be so high and then to have nothing . . .'

'Please go on,' said the journalist, taking notes.

'In Punjab, before Partition, I married into my first husband's family, Chieftains of Lahore. They had three palaces and many butlers. Servants in bow ties and frock coats.' She sighed and looked over at me. 'Not like today. Back then, everyone knew how to dress. My lady-in-waiting – a Belgian – accompanied me everywhere. We went riding after breakfast and shopping in the afternoons. We took tea at the British High Commission. Truly, we had such a wonderful time when the Britishers were here.'

'Very glamorous.'

'Oh yes.'

'Do you have any photographs of that time?' the journalist asked. 'We'd love to see some pictures.'

She became agitated. Sipped some water. 'I *had* photographs,' she said. 'But my son locked them away. What son keeps photographs from his own mother?' she went on, wiping away tears. 'Always, he's been a disappointment.'

She motioned for me to take the tray, looked at me closely. 'You're new?' she asked.

'Hahnji,' I said. 'Yes.'

She turned back to the journalist and the photographer. 'Even his servants are a disappointment.'

A pile of charred newspapers. Underneath, the caption: It's Time.

Melbourne, Australia, 1975

FRANÇOISE

All emotions are colour-coded. My mother's house was filled with the beige emotion. *Don't expect too much and you won't be disappointed*. There were the summers – the smell of bushfires hanging over the suburbs – and the children, calamine-lotioned from sunburn, jumping sprinklers in the backyard. The men would come home from work to plates of steak and pineapple and salad. Everything was in its place. My widowed mother tried to fit in, to create a wall around the family, the perfect family, in which no one could ever be sad or lonely or too independent. That's why people built fences; I sensed this from a young age. Not to keep other people out but to keep themselves in.

My grandfather and my aunty Jess were different. Jess was a nurse. She was also a hippy. 'A Buddhist or a Hindu or Age of Aquarius,' my mother said. 'Who knows exactly? You never know with Jess.' My aunt never married and she travelled widely, which was not so usual back then. Jess taught me to meditate. I was in my early teens when she came to stay. She was in between travels and jobs. In between lives, she said. She stayed for a while with her small Buddha statue and incense sticks and taught me how to breathe and how to sit straight on the cushion, how to watch the thoughts form and to watch them go.

She'd been to India and had sent a postcard of blue gods and goddesses crowding the sky. I kept it for years. She also gave me a small prayer wheel as a present.

Jess left Australia again just as things were changing. 'Look at what's happening!' she'd say. Grandpa and Jess had constant discussions. They were interested in the world. They always barracked for the underdog. They were always on the side of the people without power. The Vietnam War. The Bangladesh famine. Aboriginal land rights. You name it, they discussed it. I'd sit there and listen. The only thing they disagreed on was feminism. Grandpa didn't like hairy women, he said. Listening to them so engaged with the world was my political education. My mother had no interest in the bigger picture. She'd go out of the room when they'd start up. Every morning Grandpa would walk two miles to the Milk Bar to get the newspaper; it was the highlight of his day. He always wore a hat to protect him from the sun. When he arrived home after these walks and took his hat off a red welt lined his forehead. He'd shake out the newspaper and look at the headlines, give a section of the paper to Jess and say: 'Difficult times, difficult times.'

Three years earlier there'd been advertisements on television – girls in T-shirts with *It's Time* across their chests. A slogan song. People humming it in the street; humming across suburban lawns. We'd stayed up late in front of the TV with blankets round our shoulders, waiting for the election results to come through. We waited for my mother to come home from her work on the polling booth. Grandpa made hot chocolate and a plate of Anzac biscuits. After twenty-three years a Labour government had come to power.

Three years later, it was all over. The Governor General

dismissed the elected government. 'A constitutional coup' – Grandpa was outraged, couldn't even look at the headlines. One hundred thousand people on the streets of Melbourne, demonstrations all over the country. On television that night, Gough Whitlam, the Prime Minister, stood on the steps of Parliament House. I remember the great height of him and his voice, grey and sad: 'May God save the Queen,' he said, 'because nothing will save the Governor General.'

'Maintain your rage,' said the Labour politicians.

At school the nuns stood with their ears pressed against transistor radios, aerials up, listening to the ABC. 'Pray for Australia girls,' the nuns implored. I bowed my head and kept my eyes open, looking around the classroom. The other girls were from very different families, all Liberal and DLP voters. They lived across the river in large houses with three cars in the driveway. Their mothers didn't work. They prayed for different things.

We were sent home from school early, because of *the instability* in the country. When I got home I saw Grandpa in the backyard stoking the incinerator with magazines and newspapers. He blamed Murdoch and the media for turning against the Labour government. He burnt every Murdoch magazine he could find.

'What are you doing?' I asked, putting my school bag down and coughing in the smoke.

Those were black-and-red times. That much I remember.

❁

I moved out of home as soon as I could. For the first six years after school, I drifted, couldn't settle at anything. I worked as a

shop assistant; I worked as a plant cleaner in offices. I took part
in paid psychological experiments at the university. At night I
came home to my real work. When anyone asked me what I
did, I never mentioned art. It was private: haunting exhibitions
and art galleries. Always looking. Learning how to see. Finding
like-minded people. It was years before I ever finished a project. Mostly when I finished I destroyed the work. Started over.
At the end of this cycle, I was always exhilarated and depressed.
I'd take photos of my work with an Olympus OM10 – a camera
bought from a second-hand store.

   My first finished piece was sculpted in wood and paper,
based on the charred remains of newsprint from 1975. I called
it *Black and Red Days*. I also took photographs and along with
some art-student friends exhibited in a disused St Kilda ware-
house. The exhibition went well and people noticed my work.
People said they liked the photos more than the sculpture
itself. The attention made me uneasy because real artists came
from different families. Real artists go to art school. I was in
preparation for my real life, I knew that, but had no idea when
it would begin. One afternoon, towards the end of 1984,
when it was settling in to summer and I was home for a visit,
my grandfather held up the newspaper as soon as I walked in.
He called me over and said, 'I want you to see this, to understand the kind of world we live in.' He pointed to a
photograph of a dead child. An unknown child in Bhopal.
There was another photo of rows of bodies in white sheets.
'They couldn't get away with this here,' he said. 'A white baby
in the dirt? People living near a factory wall? No bloody way.'
He kept talking but I was fixated on the photographs. That's
when I realized the power of an image to tell a story. To evoke

what isn't there. To move people. And I realized that this is
what I wanted to do.

○

Late one night on a St Kilda street it all came into focus. Still
now, sometimes, I spool it through. How the man came from
the front, running, a man of average height, a long loose stride.
Just a man out running. At the last moment he turned, and
everything turned. Later, there was the warm room and the
police. My boyfriend, then the doctor, but I didn't sleep properly that night or for the next five years, and eventually left the
boyfriend and that life behind.

It takes less than a minute to love or kill a person. A shutter-
click of time. That man taught me this.

The attack left a scar under my right eye. Men often asked
me about it, intrigued, and sometimes I told them the story. It
made them uncomfortable, made them shift in their seats and
sometimes, it pleased me to see it.

Years later I'd look back on what happened and be thankful,
almost. That man was some kind of messenger: *You must change
your life.* After that, I heard everything differently. I looked
around the flat at all the objects collected and fashioned and
threw everything out. Then my grandfather died, the one
person who had always supported me, who'd encouraged me.
I decided I had nothing to lose and enrolled in art college, one
of the older students in the class. I studied sculpture and pho-
tography. I worked in bars and other jobs to support myself. I
worked hard. 'There's no money in being an artist,' my mother
said. 'There's no future in it.' On her monthly visits to my

Elwood flat she'd cast a cold eye over the half-finished drawings and at the makeshift darkroom in the laundry. She'd look around at works in progress, at my black-and-white prints on corkboards, and wonder aloud if I had any talent.

I kept working. *One day, you'll see*, I said to myself. *One day*.

I moved from traditional forms – wood and clay and bronze – back to found objects, to my joyous childhood habit of collecting. I carved animal bones into various shapes: fans, garlands and flowers. Cleaning, carving, embellishing. Working from death back into life. I worked with rope and sequins and velvet. I worked as if my life depended on it. I collected bits of driftwood and the skeleton of a bird. I used old masks and covered them in luxurious fabrics; rich blood-red velvet and gold Thai silk. I worked with bone, lace, beads and glass. I took photographs of these found objects, playing with filters and different paper. Cyanotype. Ambrotype. But it was in black-and-white that I could hear all the colours. The world seemed clearer.

Still, I hedged my bets with sculpture until I saw a portrait of my grandfather. My mother had found it in a drawer and given it to me. It was an old photograph of him in uniform, taken before he went off to New Guinea. A sepia-tinged studio portrait. He is young, thin and handsome. His eyes are full of the future. Looking at it, I recognized what it was that we see in all photographs, what exactly it was that set me on my path. It is the ability of a photograph to stop time. The terrible ability to call up the dead for us.

Then I moved away from sculpture altogether.

My first solo exhibition attracted attention. Black-and-white photographs which had the feel of colour. I won a major art award and was proclaimed an overnight sensation. It left me exhausted and confused. I'd promised way back that one day I'd make something out of all this. My mother attended the exhibition and admired the bouquet and the cheque I'd been given. She sighed a blue sigh and said: 'You'll always have this to remember.' As if this were the end and not the beginning. As if she were attending a funeral. 'It's a strange feeling,' she said, in a smudged voice. 'To see a child of yours, up there. It's strange. I don't expect you to understand.'

The day had come and gone, and it meant nothing to anyone but me. I returned home to my studio after the ceremony and cried myself to sleep. I cried above all for the acclaim of the one person who could never give it.

Not long after this, I met Jack. My friends thought it odd that I fell for him – an engineer, so different from me, ten years older. I'd had plenty of relationships by then. I was a serial leaver and I liked it that way. I wasn't interested in anything serious, but there was something about him. He was good-looking; everyone said so, with his dark hair and very blue eyes. He had intensity about him. He was smart and steady. *Jack.* His name had a burnt quality. I repeated the one syllable over and over.

He was self-taught, self-made, and I liked that too. He'd been a mechanic at General Motors, a union activist in the garage. He told me about the day he stood for shop steward. The elections in the tea room, surrounded by men in white shirts and neat ties and the security guards posted at the roller doors whispering: 'We've got a troublemaker.' How he'd lost the election to a leading hand who was in with the boss. After that, no more illusions, he said. He knew he had to get off the shop floor. He studied hard, every available moment. On Sundays he'd give himself a break, get out of the city and go looking for gold around old diggings and out along riverbeds. He was someone I could depend upon, I thought. He'd once been a drinker but no longer touched the stuff. A friend from his old days at General Motors told me how Jack would arrive at work back then, hungover and raw. He'd move like a big cat through the garage, thumping the duco. 'Used to scare us all shitless,' his friend said.

Right from the start there was a push-pull between us. Something withholding about him. Something comforting and familiar in that.

On weekends he delighted in driving to barren scorched places, moving through the tea trees and the eucalypts with his metal detector or bent down near a river's edge with his gold pan. He loved the heavy waxy certainty of gold, the chasing of it. In the beginning I went with him, with my camera.

Jack had a child by his first marriage, Domenic, who came to stay at weekends. Jack was fiercely protective of the boy. Wouldn't let him out of his sight. His first child he'd lost to cot death and he wasn't about to lose another child, he said. He taught the boy all about the right shade of green for a plastic panning dish. If it were too light, the blue tones reflected the sun. Too dark, the pan took on a black appearance. Gold showed up best against a particular shade of green, he said. The little boy loved choosing these pans. He hummed the colours to himself. But of all the lessons

Jack tried to teach his son about gold, all the times he pointed out the difference between gold and other metals, the only thing the child could remember was the sound of gold.

'Like a bicycle bell,' he said.

Jack turned to me, raised an eyebrow. 'Same problem as you.'

'It's not a problem.'

'Not for you. But you don't live in the real world.'

'It's real to me.'

'Come off it.' He put down his tools and came over to ruffle my hair. 'This is why I'm good for you,' he said. 'Keep your feet on the ground.'

I'd watch as his car pulled out of the driveway. His wave, more of a salute in the mornings, and his kiss on my cheek something chill. After eight years together, we undressed with our backs to each other at night. I embraced him more tightly and listened to his breathing, the colour of snow, worried that if I stopped, our lives would freeze over.

By then I was thirty-eight years old.

My photographs were changing. Away from washed shots of barren places, I moved towards portraits. To the weathered land-scape of the human. To hands and faces. I took a tight, cropped portrait of my mother's hands as she was reaching for an ashtray. She was telling a story of what I was like as a child, how I was always reaching through the bars of the cot away from her. The memory disturbed her still. My mother's hands were long and thin and worn, full of a faded grandeur. One day too, I realized, my hands would look like this.

I got more commissions from magazines and newspapers. I started going away for extended periods.

'You're different,' Jack said to me shortly after I got back from an assignment in Prague. 'Since you started going away, you're different.'

'Maybe,' I said, running the tap at the sink, rinsing the teacup, looking out of the window at the car parts and gold pans assembled in the backyard. Looking through to my weatherboard studio and darkroom. 'That's the whole point of going away.'

I'd gone back to meditation, trying to remember all my aunt had once taught me, reconnecting with that part of myself, going back to the breath, trying to sit with my restlessness.

On a whim, without telling Jack, I applied for a residency in India. Part of the residency gave funding to do my own work. For a while I'd been thinking about Buddhist symbols and patterns. About the idea of emptiness. What I became most interested in was absence. How to evoke it. How it is when someone leaves a room or a train carriage. How it is when someone vacates a street or a life. How to narrate a story from its parts? I'd thought about doing a book.

The main part of the residency was in Bhopal, to work on a monument to the gas disaster; an international project. It was approaching the twentieth anniversary. What I knew of Bhopal, of what had happened there, was all from photographs. I learned the details afterwards. Union Carbide letting the plant run down: the water seeping into the tank, the chain reaction with the gas, the poison cloud drifting over the city. It was the fact of the images which stayed with me. The child. The shrouded bodies with number tags at wrists and ankles. The man with blinded eyes. Stored in my memory archive. These photographs had been important to me, to my development. In 1984 my grandfather and I had donated money to a relief fund. I'd been moved in the peculiar way that only Westerners could be moved, by a vague feeling of guilt by association.

We are all connected, the Buddhists say.

Around this time, I took two portraits of Jack. In the first, he was surrounded by his gold pans, looking out into the distance. In the next shot, there was only the suggestion of Jack, the flat red landscape and the gullies and the creeks and his gold pans in the foreground.

As I was shooting that day, he said, 'I'm always saying good-bye to you.'

'It's my life,' I said. 'My work. It's what I have to do.'

'Your work,' he snapped. 'You do whatever you bloody want. Never think of anyone else.'

There was the incident with his son, but it was more than that.

I'd been working in my studio, in the darkroom, putting test strips into the enlarger. Domenic was playing outside. It happened quickly; the next time I looked up he was gone. An hour later I found him, playing near the railway lines at the back of the property. As punishment, Jack hit his son hard, leaving huge blue marks. 'Stop!' I tried to restrain him. 'Stop, Jack. He's only a kid!' He left the boy crying on the ground.

I put the child to bed, rocked him to sleep. Jack waited for me in the kitchen.

'It was your bloody fault.' His fist struck the table. 'Such a great artist. Such a bullshit artist. So bloody self-absorbed, can't watch my boy for ten minutes.'

Then he grew quiet and sad. 'We could have a child together,' he said. 'Maybe that'd be good for us. Maybe that's what we need.'

I went quiet. 'You know I don't want children.'

He said: 'Why is it always about you?'

He slammed the fly-wire door and walked out, loaded the car with his pans and metal detectors. Came back hours later.

Things were never the same after that, but maybe I needed an excuse. I see that now.

'You should've had a child with him,' my mother said when it was all over.

'He already had a child.'

'But a child *together*.'

'I never wanted . . . You know that.'

'Because you think you're different. Better . . .'

'Did a child make *you* happy?'

She leant back in her chair, looked down at the floor. 'Of course,' she said. 'What're you getting at? For godsake, what now? I didn't love you enough?'

'You never seemed happy.'

'That's a lie.'

'Well . . .'

'I could've done a lot of things. Could've been selfish. But I had a child. Took my responsibility seriously.'

'So, I'm irresponsible?'

She lowered her voice. 'Always have to have the last word.' She threw back her head and laughed. 'Think you're so bloody smart.'

I put my head down. Kept quiet.

'If only you'd had a child,' she started up again.

'Like I said.'

'You wouldn't have coped.' She sat back in the chair, smiled at me. 'Let's face it,' she said. 'You wouldn't have had a clue.'

I didn't see her for months after that. Our familiar mother-daughter pattern: arguments and silences. I was by myself and renting a flat in Brunswick, just getting on my feet after Jack, wondering where eight years of my life had gone. I'd been filing old negatives when there was a knock at the door. A policeman stood there with a look on his face, his cap in his hand. Later, sitting at the kitchen table, the kettle boiling on the stove, I heard what he was trying to tell me. 'An accident,' he said. 'A head-on.' Endless cups of tea. After the funeral, I stood outside the church with my aunty Jess, who'd flown in from Vietnam. All feelings blazed through. Years later I could still hear the details of the wake in the church hall. There were the irises on white tablecloths. The plastic chairs and tables. The floor covered in yellow and white lines because it doubled as a basketball court. My mother's nursing friends drinking sherry and tea. At the cemetery I gave everyone her favourite yellow roses to throw onto the coffin and I wondered if she'd think this too extravagant a gesture, then decided it didn't matter any more. I stood there, making a show of myself that she would have hated, throwing flowers on her casket, hearing the rain-sound of them falling.

When I was clearing the cupboards after her death – my father's clothes, his old racing guides, my mother's clothes – I came across a cardboard folder full of sketches and drawings. There were some other pages with my mother's signature, over and over. Most of these sketches were from her girlhood, all dated at the bottom of the page, but some were from the early years of her marriage. I sat on my knees for a long time, holding these drawings and tracing her looped initials; wondering what became of that girl and what she'd wanted. I'd like to say this made me closer to her. I'd like to say this helped me understand, but on bad days this understanding seemed no use. The hard feelings rose up. I had to remind myself that I wasn't doomed to replicate her life, that I wasn't destined for unhappiness.

After her death, I had a dream. There was a city of mosques and lakes. In the dream, a man drifted past in a barque. He pointed to a switch. An alarm rang. His eyes were burnt hollows. He used a human thighbone as an oar. In the dream, the man was speaking to me about a child.

Shortly after, the residency came through and I went to India.

A grey sky and a grey council house. A man with his arm around a dog. A small boy tugs at the man's sleeve. A woman in a shift dress looks out of the frame, smoking.

West Lothian, Scotland, 1963

ARKAY

Away for over ten years and on my return the rain fell heavy. I'd left Mykonos and the Greek girl and I wrote to her, telling her that this was me done, that I wasn't Greek-husband material.

I wore a suit, bought for the occasion. It was expected. I knew all the village men would be in suits. I went straight from the train to the chapel. I was late and my mother gave me a look but didn't say anything, just pressed my hand and there was the priest and the bells and the incense, and when to kneel and when to stand up. It all came back. I had to walk up for communion past the coffin, and the idea of my father there, it hit me. I wiped my eyes on my sleeve and then the Mass was over. My mother, Bea, blinked into the grey light as I pushed the double doors open. As I took her by the elbow, more rain started to fall.

'We've no got umbrellas . . .'

'Nae bother, Mum.' I felt my words shift a gear, shift back.

'But the suit . . . it'll be ruined . . . He would've loved ye in that suit . . .'

Behind us the door pushed out again and the mourners filed past. People ran for their cars. Umbrellas snapped open. Voices, awkward pauses, handshakes.

'Sorry, Bea . . . Sorry . . . Sorry, son . . .'

'Thanks Esme . . .'

'Bea . . . Arkay.'

'Bobby, thanks.'

A touch on my arm and I turned round and a pretty woman kissed me on the cheek.

'Arkay . . . the rain, eh? Yer dad . . . I'm sorry, Ry was a good man.'

'Caitlin.' We hugged and then I stepped back to get a good look, and liked what I saw. 'You're looking well.'

'Looking not too bad yerself,' she said. She smiled, paused. 'Ye *sound* different though. Now, listen. If there's anything . . .'

'Aye, thanks . . . thanks, I'll let you know.'

She looked at me with one eyebrow raised. 'So this'll be you back?'

'Maybe.' I shrugged.

'But mebbe no, eh?' She was still smiling. 'I ken what you're like . . .'

'Aye.' I kissed her on the cheek, couldn't resist pressing close, although I no longer really wanted her. Not really.

Around me, the men's voices: 'Arkay . . . Laddie – ye joinin us?'

'Aye.' Caitlin stepped back, flushed and said, 'So – I'll be seeing ye then? While ye're here, I mean?'

I thought I recognized the promise in her tone.

'You'll be seeing me,' I said, as if it'd be the most natural thing in the world. I watched her as she ran for the car, one arm up over her head, protecting her hair from the rain. I watched her run, admiring her legs and ankles in those shoes.

There were people at my side, my wrong side, and so I angled round to hear them.

'Arkay. OK lad?'

'Pat . . . Bobby . . . Big Rich.' The men from my childhood. My father's friends.

'How are ye?' We clapped each other on the shoulders and looked down at our feet.

Big Rich tilted his head in my direction. 'Sounds like he's been away.' He winked, nudged me in the ribs.

It was true. Apart from a few words, a few expressions, I spoke differently now. I had to come back here to realize it. 'It happens.' I shrugged. 'Been away a long time.'

'Aye,' said Pat, and his eyes narrowed. 'Too long.'

The men all laughed. I was embarrassed and to distract myself I took the small card from my pocket, just to check, just to remind myself why I was here. On one side it had the outline of a coffin edged with numbers one through eight. On the other side of the card, in italics, it read:

Mr Kearney will please
take cord No 1.

The card felt damp in my pocket. I smoothed it down and then we started off on the walk to the cemetery, a mile and a half in the rain; the road twisted and bent away from the village. It was a men's thing here, this walking behind the hearse. The women followed in cars and I could feel my mother looking at me, thinking, *My son, the stranger.*

She'd named me Ruaridh – R. K., Ruaridh Kearney – same initials as my father. I never wanted to be confused with him.

I wanted my own name. And over time I came to be known by
the phonetic *Arkay*.

I was born with the cord around my neck, a difficult birth,
the way my mother told it. They said I was a dreamy child.
Loved programmes about travel. Loved news programmes.

As I grew, so did this feeling of wanting to escape. I was a
moody teenager – who isn't? Always up in my room, the music
loud, evasive with my answers and my whereabouts. Coming
home late with the smell of drink about me and bad rumours
at my back. At seventeen I left for Australia. The years ran and
I didn't return. My mother missed me, I knew that. She found
herself waiting to hear my voice on a long-distance call at
Christmas or Hogmanay, even if it was a voice she couldn't
recognize any more. And sometimes I'd remember and send
her a card, long after the celebrations were over.

❁

In the Central Inn with the television in the corner, the sand-
wiches and scones spread out for the wake, the men with beer
and whisky, the women with tea and sherry, we talked about my
father. I took a deep breath and decided to focus on the good
things, to let everything else go. How the old man loved walking the hills; loved taking the binoculars and naming things as
he went: birds, plants, rocks. When someone was ill in the
parish or dying, he'd say 'C'mon, call the dog and put yer boots
on.' We'd go out for an hour or so, up over the shale bings or
down the burn and he'd say, 'This walk's for John, his boy's not
well.' I was surprised to find myself enjoying these stories, these
good memories of him.

'That's the kind of man he was,' said Big Rich, sadly. 'Always a one for others.'

Aye, I thought. *A one for others*, but kept silent, drinking too quickly. Then we lifted our pints to him, to the safe passing of his soul, to all the good times.

❀

I lift a pint glass to my father's memory.

And I'm twelve years old or thereabouts, and we're fishing down the burn. We've got the rods and the bait and the beer stacked up beside us and I'm casting off, about to fling the line out over the water. He's fixing the bait on his own line and instructing me and as it reels out he turns and says, 'D'ye ever think of yer wee brother?' My line gets snagged as he says this and so we wade into the water up to our knees. Water seeps in over the top of my boots and I say to him: 'A brother?' And his voice is all slurred because we've been here a while and the drink's almost gone. We wade up the bank and untangle the line and he says, 'Aye – ye had a brother.'

This jolts me like a test pattern on the telly, and I just look at him.

'He died,' he says and the tears run down. 'A year old.' I look away, though it's not the first time I've seen him like this. I pat his arm and he says we better get back and we pack up the rods and the bait and I carry the empties up the hill in a cardboard box, and I don't think I've ever seen him so bad.

'Don't tell yer mother.'

'I won't,' I say.

'Mind.' He kneels down and points a finger in my face and I can smell the drink off him.

'I willnae.'

'Good,' he says. When we get home he opens the door and calls out, 'Off for a pint.' Doesn't even wait for an answer, and I'm left in the kitchen, shivering, looking through into the lounge. The telly's on and I run in with my wet boots, and my mother says, 'It's the Taj Mahal.' It's big and white and glowing against the sandbags and soldiers everywhere. I look at it, so beautiful, and I want to be there, somewhere different and far away from here, but before there is a war and the soldiers get to it. Then there are scenes of bony kids and I wonder if my brother looked like that and my mother says, 'Bangladesh – it's terrible. The weans . . . but ye'll catch the death,' and tells me to get out of my wet clothes and bundles me upstairs and runs a bath. I go up feeling heavy and wondering whether this brother I can't remember is to do with the baby clothes in that cupboard, years ago. When I asked my mother back then she just said 'No' and was angry. She got me away from the cupboard, slammed it shut and said, 'Don't tell yer father.' And I promised I wouldn't and the next day, when I went back to that cupboard, it was empty. Just towels and sheets. I never did find the baby stuff again, though I looked long and hard for it.

❁

The night of that fishing trip I woke up choking and wet the bed, dreaming of a dead baby. Whether it was my brother or a Bangladeshi, my dream didn't say. I got a thrashing from my father on account of the sheets, for acting like a wean. The dream stayed with me.

There was no talk of my brother again and it was like it had never been said. For a few days after, the papers were full of the Bangladesh war and it took my mind off him, and I followed it for a while in the news, kind of obsessed. The bodies and the death it gave me bad dreams. We prayed for them at Mass, and put money in the plate. Things got back to normal. Though as I got older, what with the silences in the house and the way my parents only spoke through me or the dog, I felt that maybe if I'd done more, noticed more – fuck, if I'd even *known* I had a brother in the first place – that maybe he'd still be alive, and things would have been different, happier somehow, and maybe they'd not always have been on my case.

At Christmas one time, when I was really small, I went up to my gran, and lifted my shirt. My father laughed and said, 'Go on, have a look.' They all laughed, as if it was really funny – my mottled back, my bruised arse – Christ, this was the Sixties – they'd be locked up now, can't even shout now without the Social – and I was crying, because Christ, it *did* hurt and I was only five years old. But maybe it was round the time my brother died and it was for my own good. Got to give them the benefit of the doubt.

That's how kids make sense of adults.

But somehow I knew, way back, that they were all fucked. And that if I stayed, I'd end up fucked too.

Back home after the funeral, my mother had her feet up on the stool with the brown leather cushion; the newspaper spread open on her lap. She was smoking and watching the television, curling strands of hair around her index finger and trying to do the crossword in the advert breaks. I read the Sports.

'Listen, Arkay,' she said, as she put down the crossword. 'I know what ye're thinking. I don't want ye to start. I could've went years before . . . but he was a good man, always came home, had the charm – everyone said so . . .'

'A charming drunk.' I avoided my mother's eyes. 'We both know that.'

The weekends as a child: every Sunday before Mass, my mother at the stove with the bacon and chopped liver and my father coming down to the kitchen, holding his hangover like a trophy. He'd drink the glass of juice which she'd set out for him. He'd open the lid on the saucepan, inhale deep, and then she'd drive us all to Chapel and home for the liver and bacon. This was how it was. He'd walk to the pub for a few pints and come back for a sleep. It'd be late afternoon, taking the dog out, then to the pub again, and a few more pints before bed. Me and my mother, the house all quiet, waiting for him to get back. Waiting to see the mood he'd be in.

My mother sighed: 'Ye make yer bed, ye lie in it.'

'Aye,' I said. 'Some people lie in it far too fucking long.' This urge to hurt her, it came out of nowhere, this urge to make her see everything the way I saw it. I couldn't help myself.

My mother picked up the *Scotsman* again, shook it out. 'That's enough, Arkay. Drop it now.'

'Seemed to have it sorted, though.' I was in a cruel mood. 'Pillar of the community, good Catholic, good drinker, good Celtic supporter. I could've never been those things, didn't have it in me. "Ye either stay in one place or you go," he says to me. "What we leave always draws us back." No fucking way, I said to him.'

It all came out in a rush. I'd not said these things to her before and it was a shock to both of us.

'Ye're back now, so stop it.' She put down the paper and the air contracted round her.

'Fine,' I said. 'That's always been the trouble with this fucking family. We cannae *say* anything.'

She stubbed her cigarette out, put down the paper, lit another cigarette.

'What do ye expect me to say? After he got sick, after the second stroke, I washed him and fed him and put him to bed.' She continued in a flat voice. 'He'd signal with the good hand for the bottle. I wanted to stop him, but it was his one pleasure left. And it killed him.' She paused. 'It killed him, ye understand that?'

I was looking straight ahead. I listened to my mother as if I wasn't listening, as if I was a teenager again. As if I'd never gone away in the first place. I was thinking about Caitlin. Of her pressed against me, how it'd be to kiss her and hold her and fuck her again.

'Arkay,' my mother said. 'Listen. D'ye think God'll forgive me?'

I looked over and saw that she was crying. It would've been easy to walk those few steps, put my arm round and comfort her, but I couldn't do it. Couldn't break the habit of a lifetime. 'Aye. It'll be OK, Mum.' I got up, patted her on the shoulder, handed her some tissues and left. I took my heavy coat and scarf from the hook on the back door, turned up the collar as I pushed out into the cold. I drifted back to the Railway Inn because there was nothing better to do. I ran into an old school pal who ordered us both a beer.

'Been a while,' I said to him, Little John, the tallest man in the village.

'Ahh.' Little John smiled. 'The wanderer returns. Australia, no?'

'Greece,' I said. 'Australia before . . . How ye doing?' My voice sounded strained and false.

'No bad, no bad.' Little John raised an eyebrow, indicating the row of empty pint glasses in front of him, then raised a full glass. 'Cheers. Good to see ye still like a drink.' He wiped his mouth with the back of his hand, started talking about old times, about people we both knew.

'And mind,' said Little John, 'before ye go. Dan Tierney?'

'Old Dan from the milk cart?' My throat went dry.

'Aye.'

'Well, he's no in a good way.'

'No?'

'No. Rattling like a snake when he doesnae get a drink. Asking for ye, as a matter of fact, just the other day.'

'Mebbe I'll look in on him,' I said, without conviction.

'Do that,' said Little John.

I ordered another round. 'One more thing, Johnno,' I said. 'D'ye know where Caitlin stays?'

'Aye,' he said, whistling through his teeth. He passed over a beer mat and scrawled the address on the back. 'Mind now.'

'Aye.' I grinned at him, folding the beer mat in my hand. 'Always.'

When I got home hours later, my mother was still up in front of the telly. She took in the rain-soaked clothes, the carrier bag full of Tennent's from the off-licence. She put her cigarette in a misshapen ashtray I'd made for her when I was at school; a ter-racotta bowl with NO SMOKING etched around the rim. She said in an over-bright tone, 'So, young Ruaridh Kearney, in that fancy voice, will ye tell me what ye've been doing with yerself, all these years? Are ye going to tell yer old mother *all* about it?'

I crossed the room to kiss her a quick goodnight. 'There's too much to tell. I wouldn't know where to start.' I over-enunciated just to annoy her.

Up in my old bedroom, I sat on the sagging single bed and looked out the window at the other houses in the scheme. Pebbledash. Identical. Only now there were satellite dishes sprouting like fungi from outside walls. I'd spent years looking out this window when I was a kid. Nothing ever happened. I reached into the plastic bag from the off-licence and pulled the ring on the can. The day had started with a funeral and ended with a fuck. I took a mouthful of Tennent's, then placed the can on the floor and put my head in my hands. My fingers smelled of Caitlin and sex.

Sex. The drink. Dan Tierney. It all came back, sitting on this bed, looking out the window with the rain coming heavy. I lay down, hands under my head, and stared round the room. It was strangely intact, this old room. The guitar with the broken string lay on top of the wardrobe; the Marc Bolan poster peeled from the wall; the David Bowie ripped and curled. The Led Zeppelin in a cardboard box under the bed. The Jimi Hendrix album, warped from lying near the window one

Scottish summer. Summer of '76, maybe. Everyone knew that was a good summer. This room, a shrine to adolescence. As if my mother always hoped the sullen teenage boy would come back, to make her life a worthwhile misery. Here I was, a grown man in a teenager's bedroom; in the room of a person I couldn't recognize any more.

Dan Tierney. I sat up. Took a swallow.

All those times on the icy runs with the milk van, maybe five of us boys dangling our legs out the back. Two boys stacked crates, the other three delivered. We alternated each morning, jumping on and off the van as it crawled through the village. I was always happiest in the early cold and the quiet. We unlatched the gates, slid up pathways that hadn't been salted over and put the milk on frozen doorsteps. At the end of the run I always sat beside Dan Tierney. The man would grasp my knee and say: 'Well done, laddie, well done. Record time this morning.' It felt good, that appreciation. 'Come in for a bit,' he'd say, after we'd done the rounds of the scheme, the sharp sounds of bottles on concrete, the engine humming. 'I'll put the kettle on.' I was thirteen years old. The man would come up behind me and press hard into my back, then reach past me for the tea caddy.

The first times were with other boys. A group of us: the usual. The things boys do. Out in the fields round the scheme. Billy, the older boy from up the road. Telling us how he tried to suck himself off. He showed us the pulley system he'd rigged in his bedroom, showed us how he tried to do it and boasted how often he could come. I worked a paper round and most mornings I'd pick up a few magazines – scuddie mags, we called them – and put them in between the newspapers. I stacked the magazines in a hollow tree down the burn and at the weekends I'd take other boys there and we'd lean over the pictures, breathing heavy, unzipping our flies.

The paper round finished so I joined the milk van and rotated the shifts with the other boys. On Saturdays we went to Dan's to collect our pay. There'd be beer and cigarettes. A party atmosphere, though we were all of us underage. Dan'd give us a towel, tell us to have a shower, warm ourselves up, like. His flat was on the top floor, two rooms only, a fire in the grate. He lived alone. It was so warm we could wander round in towels, and if a towel slipped open, well, Dan wouldn't take his eyes away.

Dan Tierney took to showering as well, until we were all with the bare torsos and towels. Then he started the massages, each of us in turn. Later, the boys'd joke about Dan's hard cock pressed against their thighs. He had a stack of imported porn for us to look at. Every Saturday, it gave us something to look forward to, something pleasurable and disturbing, something we couldn't talk about.

As I grew older, I had a whole other life. There were girlfriends now and group sex up the bowling green with the girl with big tits. She had a name, though we didn't ever use it. Her eyes were blank and sad and it was all over quick and I felt sorry for her, though I never let on. I felt bad for all the girls we were with. They all wanted marriage and babies and a cosy life, and who could blame them? Caitlin was my first real girlfriend and I loved her, in a way, but the village was her whole world. And from an early age I knew I wanted more than that.

Around this time I started going to discos wearing eyeliner and glitter and gel in my hair. Usually one of the girls would help. I'd wipe it all off before home, but one time my old man stumbled into the bathroom for a late-night piss and saw me standing there with the flannel, rubbing the make-up from one eye.

'Always kent ye were a poof,' he said, pushing past. 'Get out of my sight.'

❀

I reached down for another beer and then another. The more I thought on it, the more I knew for certain that I wouldn't look in on Dan Tierney. And if I ran into him on a dark night, he wouldn't stand a chance. I started crushing the empty cans, winding myself up.

Poor sad sick bastard, I said to myself, *poor sad sick bastard*.

A young man looks down from a barsati roof onto the street below. He wears an orange dhoti. He holds a neem brush in his right hand.

New Delhi, India, 1984

NAGA

I argue with the sweeper-wallah. What to do? In this colony every Memsahib pays extra to the sweeper. The streets pile high in rubbish and wild pigs roam free. The street stays half-done because the sweeper has this work in private houses and her children must be fed.

I shut the wire door. Mosquitoes buzz around the entrance as the days grow cool. I tell Memsahib: 'She's coming for one hour only.' Memsahib clicks her tongue. 'Sahib won't be happy.' Outside, the sweeper waits behind the door. Memsahib walks over to negotiate. As she passes, she looks around the room; mouth turned down, and flicks her wrist. 'Sonam – the photographs.'

And so I take the duster from its hook behind the door. I look at these wedding photographs: it's all there in the eyes of the Memsahib, her life to come as the Sardar's wife. She is twenty on her wedding day and Sahib is thirty-five. Memsahib's hair shines, combed high in the style of Punjabi wives twenty years before. Heavy jewels at the forehead, ears, nose. The sweep of dark around fearful eyes, looking out of the frame, looking out at her future.

As I dust along the line of photographs and portraits of the Sahib's family – six generations of Sardars – I hear old

Memsahib calling. It is 11.30, morning. I put down the duster. Boil the chai. As I walk up with the tray, steady the cup and saucer, I hear her telephone voice: 'We had such a lovely time when the Britishers were here.' She calls the time of her first marriage the High Days, the best days of her life. The servants in starched shirts and bow ties, the bell rung at mealtimes. 'All Lahore knew that the Chief and his family were seated for supper.' She often tells these stories. I know them all. 'Now, of course,' she says, looking at my too-long trousers as I knock and enter, the loose T-shirt, my scuffed chappals, the clothes from foreigners who have stayed in this house, 'it's an entirely different matter. If my son were rich,' she says, 'they would all be in uniform.'

'Memsahib.' I look at her feet as I remove the tray and leave the room. I have mastered the art of feet-looking, of seeming other than I am. Only Sahib is not convinced. Only Sahib tries to catch me out. As I leave the room, I hear the telephone click and the dry sound of pages turning, a china cup placed on a saucer.

The doorbell rings. From the wire door, I see it is the post-wallah. He tells me through the mesh screen that a parcel has arrived for Sardarji.

'Where is the parcel?'

'At the post office.' This post-wallah is always trouble. He cracks his knuckles, he cannot keep still. He extends a hand, pleads with me. 'Money,' he says, looking around, wiping his nose with the back of his hand.

'Money?' I repeat. 'But Sahib . . .'

'What to do?' pleads post-wallah. 'Everyone is doing!' He tells me that his father found religion, left the family to become a sadhu and is now living in Rishikesh, begging alms in the street. 'My father is brainwashed,' he says. 'All family money is gone.' He is the eldest son and must support his mother and his sisters. 'My father wants me to touch the feet of his guru. But I refuse.'

I look at him closely. *Feet touching*? *Post-wallah is a Brahmin*?

'This guru bleeds us of money,' continues the post-wallah in a higher pitch now. 'I must charge more to deliver.'

'Ek Minut,' I say, stepping back from the wire door. Upstairs again to Sahib. I knock loudly. 'Post, Sardarji. Parcel at office.'

He calls me in. He's lying on his side, massaging his swollen wrist. 'How much?' he demands, not turning, still holding his wrist.

I tell him, but Sahib is suspicious. 'Last time . . .'

'Always going up,' I say. 'What to do?'

'Bloody rascal, that post-wallah.' The Sardar rouses himself on one elbow, his face red.

'Sardarji,' I say calmly. 'All post is charging.'

He motions me over, takes a key from a silver chain around his neck and unlocks the top drawer of the bedside table. He takes out his wallet and throws the money on the bed. 'Tell him to bring the parcel – now!'

'Sardarji.' I nod, taking the money. I walk downstairs and give the rupees to the post-wallah and keep some for myself.

One day Sahib says unexpectedly, 'Death is easy, Sonam. You breathe out and then, one day, you don't breathe in.' Sahib is not old, but the arthritis pains him. On bad days, when his arms are sore and the skin full and twisted at the joints, when his voice is loud and hard, I think of the day of his last breathing. How I will enter his room one morning, some years in the future. I can see myself, older, walking in. The mirrors covered, the room dark, the Memsahib gone early from the bed, not knowing. His voice an echo, only. Later I will place his photograph along with the portraits of six generations of turbans and beards and heavy eyes.

Maybe then I will go back to Tibet, to the birthplace of my family, this place I've never seen. In my dream of the Dalai Lama I always say to Him: *You must return first. Then I will follow.*

Along with the books and the clothes, some firangi guests give me money. I sew the rupee notes into my shirt seams. I save for my family in Bhopal, Madhya Pradesh. Count off the days and the weeks. In six months more, I will see them again.

The day starts well. The Sahib is in a good mood. I unfold Memsahib's winter shawls; there is the smell of mothballs as I move them from the top cupboard. I hear Old Memsahib calling for me. As I knock at her door and enter, the radio in her room crackles. 'Turn it up,' she says. 'World Service.' English words vibrate across the room. She leans in, cupping her hand around her ear.

I turn to go, the tray in my hand, but she motions me to stop. I stand in the doorway. 'Sonam,' she says, her face serious. 'Wait.' Again, leaning forward. 'Sonam! *Gas kaand.*' She pauses, looks up at me. 'The Carbide.'

'Gas kaand?' I repeat.

'Yes,' she says, then in English, to herself, 'Gas disaster.' Leaning forward again. 'This morning.' She strains to hear. She looks at me.

I stare at the radiogram, at the rug on the floor, and bow my head to the Old Memsahib. I close the door and walk quickly downstairs with one thought only.

I knock at her office. 'Memsahib,' I say. 'I must go to my family.'

Memsahib opens the door, stems of bamboo in her hand. She shakes her head. She is upset. 'Sonam. I've heard the news.' She puts the stems in a vase and steps back, tilts her head to one side and checks the arrangement. 'And I'm very very sorry.' She picks up a knife, cuts more stems. 'But what to do? Tomorrow, my son comes from America. You know this.'

'But my family,' I plead, and the tray slides from my hand. The cup and the teapot. The milk jug and the strainer. I watch it all in slow motion.

'Sonam!' Memsahib bends to retrieve the cup. Everything else is in pieces on the floor. 'You work for *our* family,' she says, her voice firm. 'We need you. Be reasonable. You can't leave now.'

I stay quiet. I pick up the tray; sweep the tea leaves and china into a napkin. Memsahib helps me. I move as if underwater. But I have made my decision. I will wait until midnight in my barsati room. I will wait until the whole house is sleeping. Then over the wall and down the fire escape, the steps rusting in my hands. I will wear the shirt with the money tight-sewn into the seams. I will get a rickshaw to Old Delhi station and a ticket on the Shatabdhi Express.

BHOPAL

A monk spins a prayer wheel; he's dressed in saffron robes. He walks past the rusting hulk of a factory.

Bhopal, Madhya Pradesh, February 2004

FRANÇOISE

I stayed a month in Delhi and then headed north to Madhya Pradesh, for my residency. Aruna urged me to take the photograph of Sonam. 'But he would look different now.' I was reluctant. 'It's almost twenty years. Do you even have an address?'

'His family lived in Old Bhopal,' she said. 'Near the factory. That's all I know.'

'Maybe he doesn't even live there any more.'

Aruna pressed the photograph into my hand. 'Maybe not. But someone might know him. He left so quickly.' She gave me an envelope full of rupees. 'We owed him wages. Please, Françoise. If you see him . . .'

'I can't promise anything.'

'Please.'

'OK. I'll see what I can do.'

'Thank you,' she said.

❀

The capital, Bhopal, was beautiful. It was the end of a hot summer and the city reminded me of the Mediterranean, the lemon and terracotta buildings edging the lakes, the frangipani

trees and the balconies full of jasmine; the cool breeze skimming
the water in the late afternoons. The remains of an old fort
crumbled gold above the upper lake.

The Rajiv Gandhi Bridge linked the old and the new towns.
The new town was all hospitals and banks and modernity. The
walled city of Old Bhopal was altogether different. It was
labyrinthine and noisy and the lanes and alleyways narrow and
full, lined with different stalls. Women in traditional dark
burquas moved heavily through the market carrying flowered
string bags. Men with moustaches rushed past on small scoot-
ers. As the day wore on in the old town, the dust and pollution
made it hard to breathe. There was an acrid taste, dun-coloured,
at the back of my throat. I took photographs of the faded buildings and the mosques and the people. I used a high-speed film
with a low shutter speed, blurring the action and movement.

I treated myself the first few days, staying at the Noor-us-
Sabah Hotel. It was a former palace built in the 1920s for the
eldest daughter of the last Nawab. I had breakfast on a terrace
next to the swimming pool looking out over eighteen acres,
New Bhopal spread beyond that. 'It's so lovely,' I said to one of
the elderly waiters. Despite myself, I said: 'It's hard to believe
anything bad ever happened here.'

The old waiter clicked his tongue. 'You are meaning gas kaand?'

'Yes.'

He paused and said sharply, 'But who wants to speak of this
past?'

'I'm sorry, I . . .'

'Here is very beautiful.' His tired eyes gazed out over the
lawns and the pool. 'But I lived in old town at gas kaand. No
telephones. Only feet like drums to sound the alarm. And gas

is staying on top of lakes for days, for ten, maybe twenty days. The gas is coming from trees and plants.'

He was so direct that it caught me off-guard. 'It's hard to believe now . . .'

He set down an old-fashioned toast rack, a small saucer of marmalade and chai in a white china pot. 'It is exactly this thing,' he said. 'Exactly what government and the Carbide want us to believe. *It never happened.*' He clicked his tongue again. 'But it did. This is what I'm telling to you.' He poured my tea, adopted a different tone.

'And how long will you stay,' Madam?

'I'm not exactly sure . . .'

'Stay and learn,' he said. 'There is much to learn.'

'Yes,' I said. I reached into my bag for my purse and saw the photograph from Aruna. After I paid the bill, I brought it out to show the old waiter. 'Excuse me,' I said. 'It's a long shot. But I wonder if you recognize this boy? He would be much older now.'

The waiter looked at the photograph of Sonam.

'He is a missing person?'

'No. Not exactly. Twenty years ago he left Delhi. He came to Bhopal after the gas disaster, to look for his family. We don't know what happened to him.'

The waiter shook his head, handed back the photograph, started clearing away plates and dishes. 'Madam,' he said sadly. 'There were many like this.'

When I left the hotel, I went to the studio rented for me in New Bhopal. My neighbours came to introduce themselves, including Shahid, a sculptor who had a studio three doors down. On this residency, foreigners were paired with Indian artists. My photographs had a sculptural quality, the organizers decided. To promote work across artforms they chose me to work with Shahid. He was fifty years old. Lean and handsome, with wild grey hair and dark eyebrows. He rode around town on an old Kawasaki and never wore a helmet. He stood there in the doorway, checking me out. He told me straight up that I should get used to the idea that our work could come to nothing.

'It depends on so many things,' he said. 'Politicians. Funding. The international situation. But . . .' He paused. 'What are your plans?' It felt more of a challenge than a question.

'Other than to take photos, document our process. A joint exhibition . . .?'

'Before all that?'

'I'm not sure what you mean.'

He raised his eyebrows. I could see he wasn't pleased with my answer.

'Well, now that I'm here, to be honest, I feel a little over-whelmed.' I thought of the old waiter and the stories I already knew. The atmosphere of the place. The photographs already taken. 'I have no idea where to start.'

'Look and learn,' he said, echoing the old waiter. 'Start there.'

Shahid was brusque, but he was also generous and funny. His studio was a meeting place in the evenings. I was slowly drawn in by the stories of the journalists and activists and artists and Shahid's two ex-wives and children who came by, all on good terms. 'Stay,' Shahid would urge. I'd stay for a while, enjoying the late-night sessions over whisky and vodka and Kingfisher beer.

The talk turned inevitably to politics. Many of Shahid's friends had lived in Old Bhopal on the night of the gas. They told me how the sirens had been turned off. How the company issued no warning until 3 a.m., more than two hours after the gas leak began. That the company refused to identify the content of the gas, saying it was a trade secret. It was like teargas only, they said, and no antidote could be given. Shahid's friends told me how they ran out into the streets along with all the others. They spoke of the gas cloud, and the wind, and the falling people who'd lost control of their limbs, dying where they fell. MIC gas caused the lungs to flood. All of them lost somebody that night and the ones who survived now worked at Sambhavna, the community health clinic, or with the gas-affected women's group or on the local newspaper. It affected everyone in different ways, Shahid said. Some had breathlessness, pains, fevers. For women there were gynaecological problems and birth defects. Many had *ghabrahat* – psychological problems. He had a friend, a writer, Mahmoud, who'd turned to drink since the night of the gas. Shahid shook his head: 'He doesn't write much any more.'

Shahid worked in stone and marble. He was working with a large block of black marble, shaped like a lingam. He'd got it from a village near Sanchi, he said, from a stream running through a Maharajah's land. People there had worshipped these phallic-shaped rocks for centuries. I picked up my camera as he prepared to work and I had a perfect shot. He closed his eyes for a moment and raised his hands, spread his palms flat. 'I'm about to alter the destiny of this stone,' he said. He opened his eyes and winked at me. 'That's what the West loves, isn't it?' he asked. 'A little Indian mysticism? Isn't that why they come?'

I laughed. 'Maybe. Some of them. Not me. I came here to work.'

He smiled. 'OK. Point taken. But in any case' – he paused – 'I believe that everything *does* have a pre-existent story. We can shatter or change or enlarge upon it. Our role is to uncover the stories in things.'

I learnt a lot that day in his studio watching him work. Over time I came to understand what he meant. Stories were out there waiting to be told. Forms were out there waiting to be filled. I could capture or illuminate some of this. Bhopal, in any case, was an ongoing story. I was learning other things too. How all events affect us at the small, private, even cellular level. And what was my responsibility, as a Westerner, for what happened here?

'I've come here, and I thought I understood, but I haven't thought it through,' I confessed to Shahid one day. 'I realize that now.'

'You're not the first,' he said in a flat voice. 'But you can help to document the city and its changes, its people, also its link to the past. More have died in the years since 1984 than at the time of the gas. They're still dying. Of respiratory infections, cancers, tuberculosis. You need to slow down and absorb all this. Take it slow.'

'But I'm only here for a short time.'

'Slow is best. Believe me.'

'If I go any slower,' I tell him, 'I'll be horizontal.'

'Slow is best,' he repeated. Then, sharply: 'Listen to the stories.' He looked up from his work. 'The West never listens.'

'But I'm not the West,' I shot back. 'I'm just me.'

'A Westerner.' He shrugged.

'We're not all the same.'

'You'll have to prove it.' He was smiling now.

'We're not all the same,' I repeated, unsure of myself, unsure of everything, shivering a little as I wrapped the shawl around my shoulders. Wondering what I was doing here.

Shahid appeared at my door the next afternoon, two bottles of Kingfisher in his hand.

'Let's go for a ride.' He was full of good cheer. 'Let's go have a picnic.'

'Shahid,' I said, 'I'm not really in the mood.'

'But we should talk.'

'So, talk.'

'Can I come in?'

I opened the wire door and he came in and sat down, swatting mosquitoes. I lit a citronella candle. 'Look,' he said. 'I know I upset you. I don't think you understand. Local artists worked hard to get a memorial project. For years. Only now it happens because of foreign money, because it involves foreign artists. I'm sorry if I took it out on you. But in general –' he grinned – 'the West doesn't listen.'

'In general, yes. But – bloody hell – I'm not an official representative.'

'Maybe not,' he conceded. 'But we all make generalizations. All Indians are computer buffs or Bollywood millionaires. Or all Muslims are terrorists. Do I look like a terrorist to you?'

'Of course not.'

'Good. A Sufi shouldn't look like a terrorist.'

'But . . .'

'Yes?'

'But . . .' I pointed to the bottles.

'I drink. Sure. I have my own beliefs. My own ways. But the point is, we all make generalizations. So,' he said, 'let's go for a ride!' He put the bottles of Kingfisher on the floor.

I pointed to his motorbike.'On the Kingfisher Express?'

He laughed. 'The West has a sense of humour.'

The next morning, I took an auto-rickshaw around the perimeter of the Union Carbide plant. I shot its rusting panopticon, its bleached and dying grasses, its upturned metal canisters, the barbed-wire fences. I looked for different angles. It was its own monument and mausoleum. Part way around, the auto ran out of fuel. 'You must walk,' said the driver. 'What to do?' We were stranded in Jayaprakash Nagar, one of the slum settlements – bastis – in the shadow of the plant. I had to walk a kilometre back through the basti to get to the main road. People came to their front doors, if they had doors, to look at me. Some of the looks were curious, some were blank, all were without malice. Barefoot children ran behind water tankers trickling fresh water. I saw women at hand pumps with plastic bottles. Many of the children had distended bellies and thin limbs. Many of the people had eye infections. I walked through this area, self-conscious, mindful of the camera and notebook in my bag. Mindful of my status as a tourist, as a voyeur, as a Westerner.

Up ahead I was surprised to see a Buddhist monk. His maroon robes caught the dust. He walked slowly, as if in meditation. Heel, toe, carefully placing each foot down. He walked purposefully through the basti. I followed him down a side alley and we emerged at the front of Carbide's main entrance. He crossed the road and walked over to a sculpture directly opposite the factory gate. It was a huge sculpture of a woman shielding herself and her children from the gas – huge, rounded limbs, like a socialist realist work. It wasn't an official monument, but a private one – the only one in town. The inscription read:

NO HIROSHIMA

NO BHOPAL

WE WANT TO LIVE

The sculptors' names were under the inscription. I walked over to the sculpture for a closer look. I stood opposite the Buddhist monk. His head was bowed. Then he raised his head, smiled at me, and bowed his head again. Up close I saw that he had purple marks on his face, like bruising, or a birthmark. I kept the camera in my bag but I took out my notebook and began sketching the figure. We stood in silence. From out of nowhere, it seemed, a group of men gathered around. The monk looked up.

'Journalist?' one of the men asked, pointing at me, and I shrugged, not understanding. I looked over at the monk. 'American?' the man continued. The monk translated for me. 'No,' I said. 'Australian. A photographer.' The monk repeated this to the men. Uncomfortable with the attention, I asked him, 'Do you know what it's made from, the statue?' The monk turned to ask the men, who responded with a volley of words and gestures and then moved off. The monk looked at me and smiled a sad smile. Translated for me again. 'The men said, "Who cares what it's made from? Thousands died here, this is what matters."'

I took a step back, closed my notebook. 'I'm sorry,' I said. My face hot. 'I understand.'

The monk looked at me, spread his palms wide. 'It is like this only: Americans come, journalists come, politicians come. Dow Chemicals buy Carbide. But, after twenty years, where is the money for medicines? Who will clean this site?' His voice rose. He shook his head. 'I come today and every day these last weeks because my sister is dying, slowly, from the gas. I walk around the plant to pray. For her, for all those who suffer.'

I didn't know what to say. 'I'm sorry,' I repeated. A rickshaw slowed down near us and I put my hand out. I asked the monk if he needed a lift.

He shook his head. 'No. Thank you.' He pressed his hands together in namaste. 'I must stay a while longer.'

NAGA

The Carbide plant was north of Hamidia Road in Old Bhopal. When I got there, the mosques and the alleys were quiet. It had happened quickly. Water entered the gas chamber. It poisoned the air: streaming eyes, the tulsi plants dying, the leaves of the peepul tree gone black. There was the smell of chillies that night, people said. People woke coughing in their beds. No one knew what was happening. A wind blew. In the telling it became an evil wind full of intent, full of the gas. It eased down one side of a street and not the other. Women fell, dressed in their fine clothes for a Sunday with jasmine in their hair. The scent released as they hit the ground.

My family were sleeping. They lived close to the Carbide. When a neighbour called they ran out of the hut. It was early morning, still dark, and cries of *Bhago, Bhago – Run, Run –* rent the air.

❖

Days later there were still chalk-white cows and buffalos upturned in the street.

Parents in New Bhopal watched their children playing hopscotch with hands over their mouths as gas oozed from trees, from plants, from the clothes of the dead. The whole city exhaling poison. These families left for Bombay, Calcutta, Delhi. Anywhere they could think of.

Bho-pal. As I walked, I called the name of that city and summoned it, in all its incarnations. In New Bhopal, high up on the hills, the Palace of the Begums rose over the upper lake; a clear sky hazed at the horizon, curved fishing boats like old barques floated at the water's edge. As if the Begum still slumbered inside her silver palanquin, moving through the town. As if nothing terrible could have ever happened.

High up in the Shamla Hills, the Carbide bought these lands and this Palace. They built new offices on the site, a huge white-stoned building. When the full moon was up, a white shadow loomed large over the city.

Always there was that shadow, people said.

There were stories of survival. One family, out near the railroad tracks, running in the opposite direction to the wind. They tied wet dupattas and scarves over their mouths, kneeling and praying, out past the railway tracks. Hours later, with the stationmaster dead and bodies on the station platform, there was no other moving thing but this family – the only survivors in the basti. Years later in the chai shops near the station, there was still talk of this miracle.

Many turned pagaal – crazy – from that night. People blamed the gas kaand. Many were ill and stayed ill. But even worse was ghabrahat, the mind suffering. The heart-speeding, wet-terror body of the survivor. Why were some spared, why not others?

For myself, I knew I was lost. In my head, the voices: 'What life is this? Struggle and fire and toxic air? Burdens that are not your own?' At night I'd leave my sister alone in the hut. I'd shut the door and walk and walk a long way with my ruined feet, hoping to exhaust myself. I limped through the bastis, out along the railway tracks, out to the lake or into the forest. Early evening along Hamidia Road away from the old city, I'd pass gas-blind women selling soft toys from handcarts; I'd weave through goats and cows and bicycles and young children with outstretched palms. I looked everywhere. Sometimes, I thought I saw them. Sometimes, my father. Sometimes, my mother. There were many nights like this. Six months after the gas kaand, I left my sister in the care of a good aunty. I took a bus to Sanchi, place of the ancient Buddhist stupas, a place I'd never been. Maybe the quiet, I thought. That day, I floated in and out of myself. When I got to Sanchi, I walked up to the stupas and round and round in a clockwise direction. For five days, I neither ate nor drank until I fell down in front of the main gate.

I lay on the ground. I spiralled away from a white light, a terrible, beautiful light which hurt my eyes. Then smoky light and a roaring wind drew me down. There were people moving in all directions, darkness beyond that. People running, stumbling, then falling. The noise of a thousand wind chimes and thunder.

'Buddha Amitabha,' I prayed. 'Help me.'

I am small and bloody and finding it hard to breathe.

There's the smell of rotting vegetables and the air stings, as if a million chillies are burning. We are running, at the hour of my birth we are

running. There is no hiding place. My mother, still holding me, stum-
bles in the gas cloud. The press of people lifts us and carries us along.
My mother loses a chappal. My mother runs with birth-blood down her
legs, with one chappal she runs, drawing up her sari, and I've stopped
screaming into life. And for some seconds, before the darkness, before the
fever hits and my burnt eyes roll back, before my mouth slackens at her
breast, I wonder where I've fallen.

Hours later, I become famous. A photographer happens upon my burial.
He snaps the adult hand caressing my forehead. My opaque eyes open, my
curd complexion, my mouth startled, my small distended body pushing up
through the dirt. I am number 2052. There is no one left to claim me.

I woke up on the road outside the stupas; a lone cow nudged
me with her dark nose. When I moved, the cow got to her feet
and I turned my head to watch as she swayed into the distance.
I lay there, imprinted on the road, the shadows long. I closed
my eyes and woke again to the sound of chanting. Two monks
from the Sanchi Monastery were lifting me up. 'Have you seen
the child?' I asked them. 'Have you seen the child?' I closed my
eyes again and humanity pulsed through. People ran in all directions. Vultures squadroned in a forked tree. Houses stood with
doors open. Overnight, the graffiti: CARBIDE QUIT INDIA. On
the gates outside the factory, in large letters: HANG ANDERSON.

'A dream,' the monks said. 'A vision, maybe. Rest now. You
must to rest.' The monks took me back with them, clothed me,

fed me, taught me to read properly and to write, gave me some measure of peace and purpose. They listened to my story. All of it. 'It led you here,' they said. 'Give thanks for this.' Slowly, I began to sit with myself. To sit with the patterns of my life. I thought of those early years on Annapurna and the endless days in Delhi with the Sardar and the Memsahib. Sometimes, I'd wake before the gong sounded in the monastery, as if I still lived in the house of the Sardar, worried that the Old Memsahib would be rousing, worried that my chores were unfinished and yet another day had begun; just like the day before and the day before that. Other times I'd wake into a dream of the gas kaand in which I could never stop running.

I stayed and studied hard and on my ordination day I prostrated myself on the ground outside the monastery. I was aware of everything: the smallest connections. Blue-tip butterflies swam in the vegetable garden. A hose dripped into an irrigation channel and a garden-wallah lay asleep on his belly. Small kite hawks flew overhead.

I closed my eyes. In the bardo of this life, so many changes, so many incarnations and clues to before. One day I hoped to understand these things fully. I moved to Dharamsala to study at Namgyal monastery, to be near His Holiness.

All was change. This was the answer and the question. This was the only pattern.

A young girl lies on a funeral pyre, one leg bent up
in the flames.

Bhopal, Madhya Pradesh, April 2004

FRANÇOISE

From the window of my studio in New Bhopal I saw white cows with bloated bellies chewing plastic from the side of the road. Small egrets perched like guardians on the cows' humps. In the early morning, the domestics wiped the dust from family cars. The young office workers passed with their silver tiffin boxes, en route to the bus stop. Most mornings, I saw a beautiful man with a mane of curly hair walking his white dog around the streets. I leant out of my window with the camera and this world revealed itself.

After that first meeting, I'd often see the monk out walking to the Carbide and I'd wave to him, or stop to say hello. His name was Naga. One day I invited him to my studio for chai. We slipped into a routine after that, a few afternoons a week. We'd sit and talk and he'd ask questions about the work. I'd ask questions about meditation and Buddhism. He had a great curiosity. He was intrigued by my laundry darkroom with its black bin-liners and the heavy curtain, the duct tape over the windows and the portable safe-light glowing in the corner.

'All makeshift,' I told him. 'I like developing my own pictures. Making my own mistakes.'

'And these?' He pointed to a contact sheet full of Carbide pictures.

'These show the gap between what I thought I saw and what was really in front of me.'

Naga smiled and nodded. 'We all suffer this gap.'

He liked to look at the prints pinned to the corkboards around the room. I'd put them up there and let them cool. I found that I had to live with the prints for a while, to trace the underlying patterns and to hear what would last.

These prints were of Shahid's hands; of a guard outside the Carbide plant; of street signs and graffiti. All cropped images.

'They look like colour,' said Naga, moving up close to the prints. 'I can feel the colours in the black-and-white.'

'Thank you,' I said. 'That's what I hope for.'

'All these stories . . .' said Naga, gesturing around the walls. 'You listen well,' he said.

'I try.'

I told him about the plans for an official memorial for Bhopal. An international collaboration. Different artists working together and a memorial comprising different artforms.

'For years the government wants only to forget,' he said, 'keep foreign investors happy. But we need to remember. Because it's not over. For people here, it goes on.'

He told me about the articles he'd collected. One day he brought one of his newspaper files to show me. 'My family moved here from Nepal,' he said. 'For work. The Carbide made pesticides, "medicine for plants" they said. The Carbide came here because it is cheap. Then they ran down the factory. There was talk of moving somewhere else, somewhere cheaper, maybe

Indonesia. There were many rumours. That night, water leaks, sets off a reaction, gas covers the city.' He paused. 'You know the rest.'

There was a whole file devoted to Warren Anderson, Carbide Chairman at the time of the disaster. Naga said, 'I'm perhaps too interested in his story.'

As he flipped over the pages, he looked up: 'Who knows when justice will come? Who knows what form this will take?' He held up an article about Anderson. 'But I truly want to know. Can a man evade his karma?'

Naga handed me the file and I read that in 1991, Warren Anderson was charged with culpable homicide, and declared a fugitive by Bhopal District Court after he failed to appear. His homes in New York and Florida were suddenly vacant. He was a wanted man, whose movements were not tracked.

'Is this a fugitive?' demanded Naga. 'They know where he spent his summers. He joined the local tennis club. I'll show you – it's all here.' He found the page and continued, 'My file grows full. Anderson is everywhere and nowhere, just out of reach.' He paused and looked at me. 'Is it a bad thing, to track another man's karma?'

He seemed so troubled by the question. 'I don't know,' I said.

'Not long ago, they find this chairman. He is eighty-one years old. He is cutting roses in his Hamptons garden.' Naga laughed. 'He likes roses! Reporters called to his wife as she drove up in her Mercedes. She said: "What are you people doing here? We have guests tonight. A dinner." As she closed the car window she called back: "It isn't even catered!"'

'And after that?'

'Nothing. They always knew where to find him. But they did nothing.'

'No extradition?'

'Too difficult. Silence, only.' Naga looked out of the window. 'They want only to forget,' he said.

Naga arranged for me to meet a doctor, a former Carbide employee. The doctor adjusted the dark-rimmed spectacles over his nose and wrote down the chemical formula for MIC – the gas which destroyed his city and his reputation. We went to the Hamidia Hospital Museum and he showed me a sack of skulls, abandoned after government funding for research was stopped. 'The results were not good,' he said. 'The government too nervous.' He showed me rows of foetuses in jars. Foetuses spontaneously aborted after the gas disaster. 'MIC gets into membranes and crosses the placenta. It continues to this day,' he said. 'Birth defects in the next generations. Cancers. Uterine tuberculosis . . .'

I kept looking at the glass jars.

'And so, as you can see,' he said, 'I'm no longer a company man.'

I took notes and made a lot of sketches. Then I brought out my camera.

I had a disturbed sleep and woke early. I splashed my face with water and prepared to meditate. As I sat on the cushion I had visions of a foetus with one eye in the centre of its forehead. Another of a foetus with a hand protruding from a shoulder. Rows of children in jars, milky-eyed, staring back.

The next time I saw Naga I told him about what I'd

photographed in the Hamidia museum. 'So many women and children affected,' he said. We talked about his sister's health and about the uterine cancer which meant she could never have children. I told him how the visit to the museum had affected me. Had shaken me up. Every time I sat down on the cushion and tried to steady myself, tried to meditate, I was thrown back to childhood. My mother, turning away. My father, absent. My grandfather's voice. A charcoal feeling. Everything turning dark.

'Meditation gives space to be sad,' Naga said. 'It comes up. It will go. This is to be expected.'

I told him that I kept thinking about my mother.

'Your mother is dead?'

'Yes. Not long before I came here. And then there was this relationship, a man . . .'

'He left you?'

'I left.'

'I see.' He paused. 'Everything, all at once?'

'Yes.' I was crying now.

'Put down your burdens. Stop struggling,' he said kindly.

'I don't know what's wrong with me.' I covered my face with my hands.

'A person who rains inside is a good person.'

'But sometimes it's too much.'

Naga said, 'The rain must come. In this country, we know this. There are times we wait for rain, above everything.'

Slowly, the work began. I photographed Shahid's hands as he carved deep into the wax and the beginnings took shape. This *cirre perdue* was an old technique. I watched him mix sesame seed oil with beeswax. He insisted that I do the work with him. I said: 'But you're the sculptor, I'm the photographer.' He picked up my camera and said, 'Nothing is fixed.' He took photos at the foundry, as men sieved the wax through pieces of cloth. In the afternoon sunshine in Bhopal, I helped him move the wax from sun to shade, watched him shape it and watched the wax harden. Like the ploughing of fields, like the gathering of grain, it was seasonal work. After making the wax replica I coated it in several layers of clay. Inside the mould I inserted bamboo splints. We then swapped and it was my turn to take photos of each stage of the process. He poured the molten metal through these splints. 'It demands that you start over,' he said, 'and make a new replica each time. Pour yourself into the idea. Then we break the mould.' His eyes shone as he said this. 'The moment where it can all come undone.'

'Like the darkroom,' I said.

'Just like the darkroom.' He grinned.

We made a series of asymmetrical bronze bells. They hung heavy off the ceiling and rang discordantly. 'Bravo!' said Shahid, when he saw the final work and the photographs. 'Alarm bells.' Carved deep into the rim of each bell was the Carbide logo.

One afternoon I asked Naga if I could take his photograph. He was near the main window in my studio examining the brass prayer wheel I'd brought with me, the old present from my aunt. One half of his face was in shadow. He stood still and quiet while I got my camera.

I said to Naga, 'Let's move. I'm not sure about the light.' But he smiled and said, 'Good light or bad light. There's only light.'

I put the camera down. 'It's so easy to forget, to get caught up. To remember that great photos are about feeling, not always about light.' I took a quick reading against the back of my hand.

'Your work is also your practice,' said Naga, observing me closely as I moved around the room. 'It is your meditation. You must stay with it, whatever your mood, whatever the day brings. You must offer yourself up, in all weathers.'

I moved a stop as he turned the prayer wheel.

He went on: 'In meditation, states of mind appear and you see them for what they are. All risings and fallings. Not all of this is pleasant. But you must stay with it. The mind is aware-ness but the watcher is an illusion. Like a knife cutting itself, or fire burning itself. At least, this is what the Tibetans say.' He smiled. 'And we should know. Tibetans have sixty words for mind.'

A few days after the photo session, Naga invited me to meet his sister, Dawa. We went to her hut in Jayaprakash Nagar, in the shadow of the Carbide plant. She was lying in a dark corner next to a window, listening to the radio.

'Aap kaise hai?' said Naga, as we walked in.

'The same,' she said. 'No different.' Then she turned her face to the wall.

'I've brought a friend.'

Dawa turned back, propped herself up on one elbow. She

looked at me closely and said, 'The photographer. Naga told me.' She did not smile. Naga translated for us.

She pointed to the radio and they had a terse brother-and-sister discussion. She took the batteries out. Naga explained that they needed new batteries. But not this brand, which had once been owned by the Carbide. His sister was angry. It was always about the Carbide, he said. She turned to me and apologized and then, quite unexpectedly, she asked if I would take her photograph.

'If you would like me to . . .'

'It's good to photograph the dead.' Then she smiled. Naga looked over at me and nodded.

The room was dark and I didn't want to use a flash. She was in a lot of pain, I could hear that. She was very tense, and so I took the film out for the first shots. When she'd relaxed a little I re-loaded the film and started again. It was a good trick; it never failed.

I took the same shot, several slight variations, just to make sure. I always held a second between shots. Sometimes in my work, I liked to over-expose by half a stop. It gave skin a luminous quality. I did it that day instinctively, because I had a clear idea of Dawa vibrant against the dark; glowing into her future. Naga moved around the room, trying to make her comfortable. I took shots of both of them together. I tried to place my camera well and listen hard. I was aware, more than usual, of the exposure time truly meaning something: encompassing the past and presaging the future.

The final image I took of Dawa showed the tin walls and the rough blanket and her clear, gaunt, unsmiling face looking away from the camera. It was a moment I always honoured, when people turned away. She was focused on Naga with a fierce and tender look. It was a look that said, 'Remember me.'

She watched as I took sketchbooks and papers out of my bag, searching for a pen. I always put the date on my film cases. As I was repacking the bag, Dawa saw the photograph from Aruna. She said: 'Who is that?'

I handed her the photograph. 'His family lived near the Carbide. Many years ago. He was working in Delhi and came back here after the gas disaster. The family he worked for would like to find him.'

'Show me,' said Naga. 'There were many like this. What was his name?'

'Sonam.'

Naga took the photo. His hands tapped over the contours of his younger self. He looked over at Dawa and laughed.

'That was my name,' he said. 'That was me.' He held up the photograph. 'Look how young. Look how thin!' He patted his belly and then tapped the picture again. 'I was only a boy.'

'You were a domestic?' I asked him. 'In Delhi?'

He smiled. 'Many years ago. One of my many lives.'

Towards the end of that second month in Bhopal, Naga walked slowly up the path to my studio. When I opened the door, his face was drawn and sad. 'She died this morning,' he said. I told him to come in and to sit down, but he stood at the door. 'At the last, she said, "I don't want to die." In that moment, so true to her feelings.' He put his head in his hands. He was silent for a while and then he said, 'There is the funeral. You would maybe like to come? To take photographs, for your project?'

I hesitated. 'Your sister's funeral?'

'It would be an honour,' he said. 'You must come.'

○

On the day of the funeral I arrived early. I checked the light readings against the wall of the crematorium and waited. A number of other funerals were taking place. Every day, all over the city. Fifteen people every month from the gas, nearly two decades of such of funerals.

The street was busy with cows and trucks and taxis. So many things were moving and there was Naga with a Hindu priest and a tall Western monk coming towards me. The body of Naga's sister was wrapped in a white sheet. The priest wore a white dhoti and a single white thread looped diagonally across his chest.

It seemed the two monks knew each other well. I moved closer. They were absorbed in the walking. I knew what I was looking for. But where best to position myself? Too close and I'd lose the sense of the crowd, too far away and they'd blur and the energy would be lost.

I was looking for another element, something that would give the photograph an edge, put the monks and the shroud into relief somehow. I saw a child with a balloon walking through. I was watching the monks and the men carrying Dawa's body, and watching the child and trying to keep all the elements in balance, shooting quickly and intuitively. It could all happen in an instant, and if everything came together, I'd have a picture. I had to surrender control. Remember to breathe, to hold steady. I felt good about what I was trying to do. There was graffiti, I would see later, words which formed a ragged border for the photograph, words that I'd not consciously noticed.

I kept moving round, shifting sideways or back, sometimes only a few centimetres. I couldn't predict the geometry of it. The more static the scene (the two monks were standing still now, inside the crematorium, listening to the priest), the more pictures I had to shoot. You just never knew what would be the defining gesture.

All these decisions; minute by minute.

I photographed Naga's face as he brought the tray up, closed his eyes and touched the offerings to his forehead. The priest chanted Naga's name and the name of Naga's father, and then the Hindu rites were over.

Naga performed the Buddhist rites. He lit the torch and touched it to the pyre. She'd wanted both ceremonies, Naga had told me that.

The Western monk and Naga stood with their eyes closed. Naga said something and the Western monk bent forward a little, angled his head to the left. I took it all in, the way you can stand outside a moment and hear all the details. The Western monk was tall and thin, slightly slumped at the shoulders, the robes hung from him. He had broad flat cheekbones, Slavic almost, his pale skin freckled and golden from the sun. A crooked nose, as if it'd once been broken. He was unusual, handsome, I decided, studying the planes of his face. I took some shots of him, and then directed my attention back, watching the flames rise from the pyre. A fluting sound as one knee bent up, animated by the heat, as if she were still alive. It was the first time I'd ever photographed a dead body, or a burning body.

I can tell you that I wanted to look away, but the camera did not.

○

Naga introduced us after the funeral. The monk's name was Tenzin Dorje.

'Tenzin is fine.' The monk was Scottish and there was something about the look of his voice, a bronze colour, which I liked straight off.

We sat on the floor of the hut in Jayaprakash Nagar. A small cassette radio and a red blanket lay on a charpoy, a metal clock on the windowsill. A gas burner. A few plates and cups. Things I'd caught on my first visit. We sat on large cushions, drinking chai. Both monks sat cross-legged. Tenzin's socks had holes and Naga's socks were heavily darned. I noticed Tenzin's scalp, the dark red hair growing through, lit copper by a side lamp. He had large grey eyes and a wide smile.

He wiped his eyes with his sleeve. I looked over at Naga, also wiping his eyes. I stared at them, hard, the way I did sometimes unconsciously, thinking nobody would notice.

Tenzin laughed: 'You've never seen a monk cry?'

'I'm sorry, it's just . . .'

'Most people cry at funerals.'

'I guess so.'

'She was a good person.'

Naga nodded. 'A good person.'

I asked if I could take a photograph. I took a shot of Tenzin's sleeve, the mala at his wrist, his head turned. I took another shot of Naga also with his head turned, lighting a candle. The small cassette radio in the foreground. Dark space around them.

After the funeral they returned to Dharamsala and I went back to my darkroom. I put the photos up on corkboards around the studio. There was something about the Western monk that intrigued me, that drew me in and for weeks after, I kept looking at his photograph.

Women and children surround a leaking water tanker. They hold up plastic containers.

Bhopal, Madhya Pradesh, February 2004

KILLER CARBIDE

The old graffiti on the factory wall. The skull and crossbones underneath.

On that first visit with Naga we walked around the plant. It was run-down and choked with weeds. I clocked the three guards at the entrance. They eyeballed us as we stopped to pray for the dead and the dying at the only monument in town. It was opposite the factory gates – a huge stone sculpture of a woman and her children.

We walked back through the bastis, past the water tankers and the queues of people and the children playing near the hoses. The queues were long. There was never enough water to go around, Naga said, and some days the tankers didn't come and people had no choice. They had to fill jugs from the dodgy ground wells. I once tried the water from the hand-pump and my tongue swelled and a rash spread over my chest. That's why Naga always bought bottled water for his sister. He didn't like to breathe the air here or drink the water or to see people line up for quack cures because the real medicines cost too much.

On these visits, I checked out Naga's files. I sat on a cushion and studied the newpaper articles. His collection went way back to

1984. I read that the Indian government got nervous about foreign investment, so the Supreme Court settled in 1991 for a pittance.

In one of Naga's files there was a recent article: *When Union Carbide finally left Bhopal in 1999 waste chemicals were left behind. It denied these toxins leached into the soil and water around the factory.*

'You see,' Naga said. 'It goes on. My file grows full.'

I knew about the gas disaster from the television, from the newspapers, but I never would've gone there if I hadn't met Naga. To go there is something else.

On my first visit his sister Dawa was already very ill. It was her time of the month and when her bleeding came it was pure pain, anyone could see. Naga lit the gas ring, heated a small brick for her, wrapped it in cloth and placed it on her belly. The air stung with mosquitoes on account of the lakes. Dawa lay there with her eyes shut and Naga lit citronella candles to keep the insects away. He took his sister's feet; massaged the pressure points. He told her of our walk around the factory. He brought the world in to her.

I held her hand and the skin was raw and angry near the wrist. I heard her prayers. Each time a wind lifted the curtain she knew that night again, she said. The night as gas chamber; a wall of cloud when the clouds became walls.

On the next visit I went with Naga to the municipal offices. Each time he was back in Bhopal, Naga queued to make a claim for compensation. Most times they told him he didn't have the proper papers. Government doctors said Dawa's illness was *purely psychological*. But each time he returned and waited along with all the others. He'd learnt patience. But I was fuming when we came out the office that day. I had to stop myself jumping the counter, had to restrain myself with the government doctor.

When I told Naga this, he said, with a tight grin on his face, 'Next time – you jump the counter.'

On the day of Dawa's funeral, it was overcast and humid. Her body burnt on the pyre and one leg, blackened and twisted, came up through a rip in the cloth. Naga was intent on the flames. And I got to thinking of our time in Varanasi, three years back. The all-night vigil at the ghats. The body on the pyre. My first introduction to death up-close. There was a woman talking to Naga, a Western woman. She was tall with golden skin. She had a small deep scar under one eye. She was taking photographs.

She was good-looking, I could see that.

I looked over and she was looking at me, kind of frank and appraising, and then we both looked away. The Hindu priest adjusted the thread around his body, said something to Naga. I looked over again at the Western woman, but she'd turned to focus her camera on the priest.

In my former life, I know I would've . . . for sure, I would've tried to . . . I was following these thoughts, the snaking trail, watching them form and dissolve. I drew my attention back to the pyre. I realized that I was trying to distract myself with old sex talk, noticing the woman and so on, my mind running away from death, the old story. I told myself to stay still. Later when we got to know each other and things turned, it came back to me, how we first met. The distraction I was looking for.

A metal clock on a table. A radio cassette player on the floor. A curtain lifts in the breeze.

Jayaprakesh Nagar, Bhopal, March 2004

Tenzin came with me to Bhopal. He visited one time when my sister was very ill – without appetite and short of breath. *Uterine cancer*, said the doctors. They told her she could never bear children.

He sat and listened to her heart-story: the story of the wall of cloud; the moment they began to run. He was patient with her; he showed her great kindness.

I remember this visit as I wash my sister's feet and press the points there. Since the gas night, the feeling in her hands and feet swings between needle-pains and complete numbness. I tell her of the walk around the factory. I tell her of the foreign woman with her sketchbook and camera bags. My sister smiles. She likes that I bring the outside in to her. I now anticipate her death, steady myself for it. Each time I return there's a new symptom of this dying. The sickness takes hold. Her bleeding, when it comes, is so painful. I heat bricks over a low flame, wrap them in cloth and place them on her belly. My sister is moving from water to spirit. I hold her thin arm and see the rash near the elbow. I hear her prayers. Each time a wind lifts the curtain she experiences that night again. In some traditions, they say, if you've lived a good life death starts from the feet. Nurses make small ink imprints of the feet of dead children.

Something for the parents to remember. As I take my sister's foot and massage the points that pain her I know I will remember these moments. And already I see the outline of her foot in my memory, a small sacred imprint of love.

◇

I took Françoise to meet Dawa. It was only weeks before my sister's death.

As we knocked and entered, she propped herself up on an elbow. She did not smile. She was listening to the news bulletin on All-India radio. Then the voice crackled then stopped. 'The batteries, isn't it?' Dawa said, reaching over, turning the switch off and taking the batteries out. And then she turned to me, voice high with accusation.

'These?'

'I didn't buy.' I looked at the Eveready batteries in her palm. 'In the monastery, someone else replaces.' I turned to Françoise. 'I bring the radio with me.'

'But these?' Dawa let the batteries fall from her hand onto the floor.

'Forgive me,' I said. 'Next time, I will tell them.'

She looked down at the floor. 'Give me Red.'

'I'm sorry,' I said. 'Please.'

'Give me Red.'

Dawa looked over and apologized to Françoise.

'You see,' she said, raising herself again on one elbow. 'One time the words were everywhere. Carbide owned Eveready. After the gas kaand, it meant something different – *Give Me Red* – large banners, boycotts.'

I translated for Françoise. Dawa lay back on the charpoy, exhausted by this explanation. 'We need some new batteries,' she said to me. 'Tell me when you find.'

I moved towards a low stove and took up a brick lying near the door. I heated the brick over a low flame and, when it was warm enough, wrapped it in a cotton dupatta and placed it like always. 'Today is not a good day for her,' I said to Francoise.

And then Dawa said to me in a heavy tone, 'But maybe a good day for a photograph?'

I told Françoise and she looked at Dawa. 'Only if you want me to.'

Dawa turned to face the wall, said something about photographing the dead.

❁

The night of my sister's funeral I dream of travelling up the Ganges. I am at the ghats of Varanasi. I see Tenzin on the far bank. I see the burning bodies: the charcoal fragments in the water; the chests of the men and the hip cavities of the women that defy burning; how everything is returned there. I travel past the burning ghats. I see it all and feel calm and still as if everything is moving except myself. I put my face up to the sun and I am Aryabhatta, eleventh-century mathematician, inventor of zero. I look up; suddenly blinded by the sun's core, I feel the turning of the earth around the sun, wanting to tell the world of this discovery.

The sun, the wheel, the sphere, the zero.

Zero is the absence and the total of all things. It is the sum of and the end of the universe.

Zero is *sunya*. Zero means *off*.

That night in Bhopal, the zero was silent, switched off months before by the Carbide.

In the dream, I'm searching for the switch. I cannot find it.

Bhago, bhago. Run, run. The words shatter in cloud. People rise and fall in waves. They stumble on dust, sink into the hard earth; children are trampled and lost. Streetlamps burn faintly, like candles behind cloth. In the dream, I am Aryabhatta the inventor of zero. I am also the fallen, beyond number.

✿

KILLER CARBIDE. The graffiti always gave me satisfaction. The skull and crossbones fading on the factory wall. And then, after the company takeover, the new slogan: DOW – LIVING POISONED DAILY.

Since my sister's death, the last of our family, there is no satisfaction. Nothing brings me consolation.

I wake in the night, unsteady, and I must sit with this feeling, feel it right down, feel it burn through until it is gone. There is no escape. What is it trying to teach me?

There are two paths: to harden or to soften. To be brave with the hurt and to sit with it, not to run. To have compassion for all those who suffer as you are suffering. This is one path. Or a person can harden; can create a shell around their hurt. This is the other way: to make a pearl of the hurt and close around it.

How can I soften? Why, so much, do I want to harden?

Who knows when justice will come? Who knows what form this can take?

My own private story and the story of this city. I take out my files. I add my sister's name along with all the others. Nothing consoles me.

❁

The day after the funeral some men came to the hut, their fists raised. They are from the moneylender. He wants his interest on the loan.

'Loan?' I say.

'Two thousand rupees,' the men say, crowding the door. 'The medicines for your sister. Ten per cent interest. Two hundred rupees a month.'

'We have nothing,' I say. 'She told me nothing of this.'

'For her medicines,' the goondas say, pushing past me into the hut. They throw me to the floor. They take the one good brass pot and the brass lamp. The metal clock. They take Dawa's gold bracelet and the rings which belonged to our mother. They take the monastery radio. They take everything they can.

I do not resist. I let them take everything.

Some days after this, the people from Sambhavna health clinic come to the hut. They have come to ask questions, to take a verbal autopsy. I tell them Dawa's symptoms, her age at the time of the gas, what the doctors said. Her monthly pains. All of it. Sambhavna are the only ones to record such things, to monitor the deaths from the gas.

I tell them about the goondas. I tell them about the money-lender. How my sister kept this from me.

'All over the bastis this happens. People turn to the money-lenders.' The woman from Sambhavna shook her head. 'We

had contact with Dawa so late. People go to the moneylend-
ers and the cycle starts. She didn't want to upset you. But
people come to us and we help them. People donate to our
work. Foreigners, even. We keep going. There is no choice but
to keep going.'

'Accha,' I said.

❁

After her death all those years after the gas kaand, I queue for
the last time at the government offices. They give me money,
compensation that doesn't even cover Dawa's medical bills. Less
than seven rupees a day since the night of the gas. There is no
compensation for the death of my mother and father.

I give the money to Sambhavna. I give it to the women's
clinic.

I suffer bad headaches, the old problem. My eyes are sore.
Our Tibetan doctor says, 'It is anger. Your old friend, coming
to teach you. Try to sit with this anger.'

❁

When Françoise came to the hut in Jayaprakesh Nagar, she had
a photograph in her bag. A photograph of myself as a young
man in Delhi. We spoke of the Memsahib and the Sardar. Of
the Old Memsahib. The connections between us. Françoise
gave me an envelope of money from the Memsahib. Over one
month's wages from all those years ago. I used this money for
my sister's funeral.

Françoise often asked me about meditation and about the

monastic life. She asked whether I had any regrets about the life I'd chosen – the vows of chastity, austerity and discipline.

'In general, no,' I said. 'And this life chose me, in any case. But every life has doubt. Every life needs this element of doubt. It makes us measure our lives against the lives not taken. To see our path more clearly. This doubt,' I said, 'is to be expected. Is only natural.'

It was after Dawa's death, this conversation. I was full of doubt.

We talked of many things. It was some comfort. I told her what I'd read about the Black Sea – that at 500 metres it has no oxygen. Imagine. Its depths are sterile and all is preserved: a wooden barn; a terracotta vase; fragments of jewellery; the bones of an ox. Everything frozen. And sometimes, I confessed to her, I had that experience with people. The deeper I looked, the less I could see. Sometimes, to my disappointment, there seemed a complete lack of oxygen in the inside life.

'Of course,' I apologized to her, 'this is my judging mind. A constant struggle. It's my own inside life I must worry for.'

I told her that sometimes I could foresee things happening. Standing at a bus stop, for example, waiting, and I could see myself, older, on a bus going past, sitting there, staring out of the window or maybe reading a book. Lately, I'd seen a child sitting next to me. Something in the future.

'How long has it been like this?'

'In this way, more recently. Since Dawa's death. Perhaps because I'm getting older,' I said. 'Perhaps this is the reason.'

She looked at me closely. 'You're not old. Not much older than me.'

'But I feel much older.' I smiled at her. 'And all my lives press down.'

✿

Back in Dharamsala, the Abbot of our monastery came past my room. He saw me sorting my folders, updating the files. He stood in the doorway and pointed to the scissors in my hand, at the newspaper clippings all over the floor. He laughed at my *obsession*.

I said to him, angry, 'But this is my life.'

'Yes,' he said. 'The pain never goes. We will never be happy.' He laughed again as he said this.

I could not hear him, could not face him. I had taken the other path. I had made a pearl of my hurt and all was struggle as I shut the door. As I lit a candle and moved to the cushion.

RAJASTHAN

A bus stops near a cart with an overturned load. In the foreground there is a stall selling chai.

Road to Jaipur, Rajasthan, June 2004

He was eight rows ahead of me on the bus from Agra to Jaipur, the last person I expected to see. He slid into the first available seat as the bus moved off. I almost didn't recognize him. He looked strained and thin as though he needed sleep, and his hair was growing through. There were traces of a beard and I noticed his hands shook a little as he held onto the seat rest. I called his name, but he didn't hear me over the noise of the engine and the people crammed in the aisles and the families pulling food hampers from their luggage.

We were the only foreigners on the bus and it was late afternoon when we left Agra. A yellow pollution haze hung over the city. The bus wound through the market streets and stopped near the leather stalls. There were soles of shoes piled on the road and a smell of dead animals and blood so strong that I had to close the window.

When we finally left Agra the traffic came heavy. Trucks stormed down the middle of the road, veering off at the last minute. Small top-heavy tractors lay overturned in the gutters; burlap sacks split and mountains of grain poured out. As darkness fell, camels and bullock carts and rickshaws emerged in the centre of the unlit road, almost colliding with the bus and then, by some miracle, easing past.

A motorcycle slammed into the back of the bus. Our driver checked the rear mirror, and put his foot to the accelerator. The monk looked back over his shoulder, caught my eye, seemed confused for an instant, and then smiled a wide smile. Three hours later we stopped for chai at a roadside stall. We struggled down the steps, stiff-limbed, awkward. He waited for me to get off the bus.

'Tenzin.' I held out my hand. 'I'm Françoise . . .'

'I remember.' He smiled. 'Bhopal. But what are you doing here?'

'I'm on holiday,' I told him. 'A break from my work. And you?'

'I'm on sabbatical,' he said.

'Naga mentioned . . . We keep in touch now he's back in Dharamsala. He wrote and told me about your mother. I'm sorry.'

'My mother, aye.'

'He told me you went back to Scotland.' I hesitated. 'It must've been tough.'

'It was.'

'Being so far away, I mean.' I kept talking, despite myself.

'It came out the blue. Heart attack in her sleep,' he said. 'That was tough.'

'You were close?'

'In a way. In that Scottish way of not really talking, we were close.'

I smiled. 'And the funeral?'

'I only ever go back for funerals.' He shrugged. 'Ten years ago it was for my father, before I went to India.' He looked off into the distance. 'My mother had a good send-off. All her pals from the village were there. A fine priest. She left me some money, bit of life insurance. And here I am.' He spread his arms wide. 'After ten years in India, I've finally seen the Taj Mahal. I've finally got to Rajasthan, to the desert.' He paused and looked down at his feet. 'Anyway, it's good to see you again.'

'You too,' I said.

An empty council house. A for-sale sign casts a
shadow across the front garden.

West Lothian, Scotland, April 2004

ARKAY

I'd been dry-eyed through the service for my mother, trying to keep it all together. I'd always thought I could come and go and that she'd be there in her usual place by the fire with the cross-word. It was a child's-eye view of the world and truth is, I'd clung to it for far too long.

After her funeral things started to slide. It was the end of April, only a couple of weeks since the death of Naga's sister. Coming from India, everyone looked pale and ill. I stayed a week in the old family house; sat on my old single bed, looked out at the dreich sky and the wet streets. I moved the chair where she used to sit. I emptied her ashtrays and gave her clothes away. Did the same with the books. She'd left a will, and I spoke to the lawyer about selling the place. They'd arrange everything, they said. I didn't want to stay a minute longer than I had to. I turned on the telly. I walked to the Co-op; past my old school; past the Oaks – the pub where I once beat a man after an Old Firm game. There was graffiti on the car-park cement. I stopped to look and saw that it was the same graffiti only faded. How easy I slipped back after all this time, into this life with so many distractions. It seemed as if I'd never been away. I felt it, the discipline of the past ten years, loosening. It all started to go. I was like an office worker at the end of a long day, wanting to throw off his tie, put his feet up.

Have a drink.

And I hadn't felt like this, not for years. The occasional urge maybe, but it'd been a long time. But back in the village it was everywhere, coming at me in 3D.

My mother gone, my father gone, I'd no more ties to the place. I sat cross-legged on the carpet in the living room; I heard the central heating click on. I was there in my robes and nothing felt right. At the back of me, there was a huge space, and I was falling into it. *Ten years, like that.* I couldn't say what was happening. I'd wake in the early hours, the feel of nothing holding together, the whole pack of cards blown down. All I could do was lie there with the tight coiled feeling inside. Something I couldn't reach or understand.

No one left.

One drink won't hurt.

I dressed in civilian clothes and walked into the Central. My first pub visit for ten years. Last time I'd been here was for my father's wake. The neon slot machines, the cigarette smoke, the chip-pan smell, all hit me as if I'd never left. Little John was there. 'Back where ye belong,' he said. I couldn't think of a response. There were the same old faces at the bar. I told them I'd been in India. I told them that, aye, it was true enough, I'd become a Buddhist monk. I ran my hand over my shaved head. I told them the occasional drink couldn't hurt. I'd have one drink and then go.

Little John asked if I had a new name, a Buddhist name. I hesitated. As I lifted the pint glass I said, 'Just call me Arkay.'

'Arkay's back!' Little John toasted me, ordered another round. It was all under control, I told myself, three drinks in, and the room slowly turned amber.

I thought I knew all about death, but that was just ego talking. In India, I'd seen plenty of death, out on the streets, in the monastery. All the old Tibetans dying of TB. I'd sat in graveyards. I'd sat with burning bodies. Then there was Lama's death not long back – I'd got through it. I was used to the grim reaper, I told myself.

But my mother's death, *her* death, got me by the throat. It wouldn't let me go. It was sudden, they said. In her sleep. She was at peace. But it was no consolation, and I wanted to see her once more and maybe talk, apologize, thank her even, for all she did. Any certainty, any knowledge of my path fell away. I'd wake up early every morning like I had for the past decade, but I couldn't get to the cushion. I couldn't sit there with the dawn howling down. I'd lost my place in the universe. No country, no parents, no guru, no safety net under the tightrope. Although it was nearly three years since Lama died – it all came back – in a oner. I'd wake with my heart not sure of itself.

I called the Abbot and he urged a sabbatical. After ten years I needed some time. I could do with a break. *When I get back to India, this'll stop.* A couple months' travel, see the Taj, a rest, and then back to my old life at the monastery.

At the airport I took a detour through the bar. On the Air India flight, still dressed in civvies, I got another can. And another.

I was coming unstuck, and I knew it.

I kept up the internal chat. *Soon I'd stop.* It was possible. Of course it was. As I peeled the label from a bottle of red I told myself: *You've done it before.*

We rearranged our seats and sat next to each other for the rest of the trip. I was aware of the warmth and angularity of his body as the bus jolted over the road. He apologized each time and moved his shoulder away, adjusted his robes, looked straight ahead.

A horn sounded and I looked back. 'Oh no.' I nudged him. 'The bus behind us wants to race.'

A five-hour trip stretched to ten hours. It was late evening when we reached Jaipur. We were both exhausted. We shared a cycle rickshaw to a guest house recommended in my guidebook. The owners were black-eyed twin brothers, and as they walked up the stairs, I noticed their enormous identical feet, cracked at the heels. I thought how I could frame those feet and concrete steps. Tomorrow I'd ask them if I could take a photograph.

We settled into our separate rooms, showered, and met up on the roof balcony. I was surprised to see the monk dressed in a white kurta and khaki trousers. Five floors below the pink city was all neon signs and twisted television wires. A tangle of car horns and filmi music rose up from the streets. It was election time. A car was blasting out election slogans, and then: 'Gandhi is a foreigner. No foreigner for office.'

'What are they on about?'

'Sonia Gandhi, I think.'

'Because she was born in Italy?'

'The BJP want to discredit her. Even some in her own party . . .'

'But she's an Indian citizen.'

'Not good enough, apparently. She wasn't born here.' He rolled his eyes. 'While we're on politics . . . did you get to the Taj Mahal?'

'Uh-huh. But – I guess it's strange for me to say – it was too much like the photographs. Unreal almost. And the tomb – Shah Jahan never wanted . . .'

'To be buried there. I know. It should never of happened.' His voice was bright. He looked thinner and shadowed round the eyes. I could've sworn he'd been drinking. 'The tomb, aye. Since I was a kid, I'd always wanted to see it – the whole she-bang. Amazing. A monument to eternal love? I'm not convinced. But as a monument to eternal ego, the Taj is a fuck-ing triumph.'

Everything about him surprised me; there was an edge to him now, quite different to how he'd been in Bhopal just two months earlier. It was as if he'd shed a protective layer. Even the colour of his voice had changed a little. He took a bottle of Bosca Red from his rucksack, poured a glass for me and one for himself and we talked long into the night.

We arranged to meet the next afternoon, at the Indian Coffee House. I sat at a table by myself in a far corner of the room.

Elderly waiters in white turbans, Nehru jackets and blue cummerbunds moved slowly around to the rhythm of the ceiling fans. Their turbans topped with stiff blue paper, like peacocks' tails. Sepia photos of a rouge-cheeked Indira and a gaunt-looking Nehru hung crookedly on the walls.

As he walked in, just before the fly-wire door swung shut I saw the members of a brass band running past. Flashes of red and gold epaulettes. Tubas and horns. The band members in dirty white suits, nipped in at the back and at the sides with large safety pins. I watched them run past, trouser cuffs dragging in the dirt, instruments and turbans in hand, obviously late for a wedding. It was a common sight. It was one of the few times in India I ever saw anyone run.

As he came through the door he was laughing: 'Why the rush?' He nodded after the tuba player. 'Why always late? Every brass band, the same story.'

'I know. Always running. Take a seat . . .'

'I could murder a coffee.' I liked the way he spoke. The *r* sounds extended and low. He sat down but I was on his wrong side. 'Would you mind?' he asked, pointing to my chair. 'To accommodate the ear?' I shifted round the table, so that I was on his right. The waiter came and we ordered our coffees.

'They say if one sense is halved, others compensate.'

'Maybe,' he said. 'My eyesight's pretty good.'

'Can you see sounds?'

'No.'

'Can you hear colours?'

'Not my forte.' He was amused. 'Can you?'

'Well, as a matter of fact, yes.'

'How come?'

'I was born that way.'

'You're lucky.'

'Everyone's born that way. Apparently all babies have it. Most of us lose it as we get older. For some of us, it stays.'

'Like I said. Lucky.'

'Everyone has a way of looking at the world.'

'True enough. For me it's all about space,' he said, 'that's the first thing. Where to sit, where to stand. Can I hear everyone? Can I see everyone even if they're on my wrong side? Space is what I notice first, and angles.'

'You could be a photographer.'

He smiled. 'In another life. But tell me. You really hear in colour?'

'Yep.'

'But you work in black-and-white?'

'Fewer distractions . . .'

'Uh-huh.' He leant forward, angling his head to the left. 'What's the colour of one hand clapping?'

I closed my eyes. 'Gold,' I said.

'The sound of tea?'

'Like a rainbow,' I said without hesitation. The questions made me laugh. 'Is this a test?'

'Not a test.' He grinned. 'Just curious.' He drummed his fingers on the table. 'I know,' he said. 'A siren?'

'Green. It loops and curves. I feel it in my belly.'

He laughed. 'You're lucky. All I've got is one cloth ear.'

Then he told me how he'd come to India not long after his father's death. He told me about Naga and Lama Shastri and how he'd become a monk.

He told me he'd been to Australia once, when he was young.
Had travelled up and down the east coast looking for work.

We sat and talked a long time that day. The only firangis in
the place.

ARKAY

I see I was fierce with it, in the manner of Westerners taking to the East, in the manner of a Catholic taking to the Buddha. At first it's the relief, what you think you've been wanting – away from the village, away from what you would've become. After a few years in Dharamsala I thought I was ready for the next step – for monastic vows – ready to answer all Lama's questions.

I'm not running. I truly believed I wasn't. Something had shifted after I'd taken Refuge. Especially since my stint in Kerala. It was Lama first told me of Kerala, when I couldn't hide from him any more. Couldn't hide from myself or cover my tracks. Some monks run a programme, he'd said, and he was gentle with the suggestion. I booked my ticket, a long, long journey, and drank all the way, every desperate mouthful sure to be the last and those days and nights on the train, they all merged together. When I got there I could've turned and left, but the monks were completely unfazed. They'd seen it all before. The truth is, I was ready. For the meditation, the fasting, all of it. I shook and retched and sweated like a hostage. At the end of six weeks I was hollowed out. The monks taught us to work with the breath, to go back to it, and when the cravings rose up, to distract ourselves: to go for a walk; to speak to someone. *Not to surrender.* Only thirty seconds for a craving to pass. This is all it takes. Try to sit with it. Sit with the old mind playing old tricks. This is what they taught. I was the only jakey there. All the others had the real problems, if you ask me – heroin and the like.

Anyway. I was ready and I told myself it was no longer about escape, as if it were ever that simple. In Dharamsala, I shaved my head and moved into a small room at the monastery. Along with all the other monks I slept on a three-inch mattress and ate one meal of rice and dhal a day. I was ordained 'Tenzin Dorje'. Everyone called me Tenzin. We studied and chanted early every morning, and again in the evenings. We trained in ritual activities: the construction of mandalas or the art of painting with coloured sand. This life was happy and simple and clear. There were the old cravings but the early weeks in the monastery came easy enough. Too easy, maybe. I was high on all the changes; with leaving my old life. Like when I first took Refuge. How I thought this was me, all set. Done and dusted.

After two months it was a different story, what with all the old thoughts and the pain rising up. The harder I practised, the harder it was. Small tasks were a torture: washing the dishes or the floors, I couldn't see the point. Couldn't be doing with them. Took me away from my practice. At the time, that's how I saw it. Everything was practice, if you were aware, but I wasn't aware. My body tensed as I sat and my mind ran fast. Grew anxious when I gripped a bucket or a broom, forced myself to the breath, forced myself to the cushion, where before it'd been my comfort. My meditation was weak, my monkey-mind too active.

I wanted to blame someone, anyone. *My teacher was too strict. My teacher wasn't strict enough.*

Lama Shastri threw sudden, sharp questions like Zen koans: 'What was your original face before you were born?' I was clueless. I was miserable. He told me to sit, to wait for the answer. To rest in the space before the answer. It was like the early days with Lama, I told myself, only now the stakes were higher. He was more serious with me. I was all thrown about. At times he seemed distant and even severe. *Relax into the questions,* I told myself. My head hurt, trying to find answers.

In the evening, more questions: 'All things return to the one,' said Lama. 'So where does the one return?'

I sat straight through the night meditations, not wanting to fail. All around me the young Tibetans slumped forward, asleep. Some even snored. I stayed awake, the only one, and it felt good, bolstered the old ego for a time. I was trying so hard. Then Lama took me aside. 'So much struggle.' He shook his head. 'Let go, Westerner. Become loose.'

I struggled to become loose.

Then one morning, after another all-night meditation in which I was the only one still sitting, still awake, Lama called me over. 'Everything bothers you,' he said. 'Everything disturbs you, isn't it?' I wanted to contradict him – I'd started to feel a wee bit better, able to focus again – but he held up his hand. 'Nothing is perfect for your meditation. It's the fault of the world outside; it's the fault of your teacher.' He laughed, pointing to himself. 'Or maybe the others?' He pointed to the young monks asleep on the floor. 'Only *you* are serious in your meditation. Only *you* can stay awake? You are the best?' He smiled. 'But tell me this. When the monkey comes over the Gompa roof, does it come to annoy you, or do you go out and annoy it?'

I laughed, and for an instant there was space, no yammering *self*, just for a minute, before the next thought came in.

When I loosened up it got easier.

Those years in the monastery – the flow of them, so smooth they seemed when I looked back. The clean mountain air. Everything clear and simple. In the mornings, I'd watch as the first young monks appeared on the balcony, emptying water from metal pots, I'd watch as the water slow-arced into the courtyard. For ten years that routine. The gong called us to meditation. Up at 4.30, then wash, fetch a glass of hot water and a cup of chai from the kitchen. I chanted and studied hard. There was the music – the drums and the conch and cymbals. In the morning and the evening there were the texts. For years this was the unvaried pace of my life.

It kept me on the straight and narrow. I clung to it. I didn't want to lose it.

After the first five years there were fewer thoughts of the drink, even fewer thoughts of women. It got easier, the longer it went on. This was my life, my path, I thought to myself. *This will be the way of things. Forever.*

A monk sits cross-legged on steps leading to a well.

A woman in a sari bends down to light a candle.

She floats the candle on the water.

Jodhpur, Rajasthan, July 2004

FRANÇOISE

He told me he'd been briefly married – in Australia – when he was young and travelling around. It was long ago, he said. They divorced way back.

'Where did you go in Australia?'

'Here and there. Up the east coast.'

'Melbourne?'

'That's where you're from?'

'That's right,' I said.

'Went there once.' He hesitated. 'To tell you the truth, I don't remember much.' He paused again. 'Too long ago. But what about you?'

I told him I'd come to India a few months after the end of a long relationship. How my mother had died and that everything seemed to happen in a short space of time. How overwhelmed I'd felt when I first got to Bhopal.

'Of course you'd be overwhelmed,' he said. 'The whole she-bang. You've seen Naga's file?'

'Uh-huh. Even if they get Anderson, it'll take years, if ever, for proper compensation or to get the site cleaned . . .'

'And in the meantime?'

'There's the community groups. The activists. Then there's the memorial project.'

'Step by step.'

'I've made a start with the work. But if you stop for a while and there's no distraction,' I sighed, 'then life catches up with you. Overwhelms you. Work is a great distraction.'

'So, rest. Relax,' he said. 'Maybe that's what you need to do.'

'If I rest any more, I'll never get back.'

He laughed, took a sip of his coffee. 'How long were you together? The relationship, I mean . . .'

'Eight years,' I said.

'A long time.'

'And how long have you been a monk?'

'Ten.' He twisted the mala on his left wrist. 'But eight years,' he said, 'for a relationship, that's a lifetime.' He raised his hand as the waiter came past and we ordered another coffee.

❁

I asked him what his name was before he became a monk.

'Arkay,' he said. He spelt it for me.

'Sounds Indian.'

'It's from my initials – R. K., Ruaridh Kearney.'

'And what about your monk name? What does it mean?'

'It means: "indestructibility, compassion and skilfulness".' He shrugged. 'I could never live up to it. Lately I've gone back to my old name. You should call me Arkay.'

'If you want me to . . .'

'I want you to.'

He asked me how old I was.

'Thirty-nine,' I said. 'Actually, thirty-nine and a half.'

'Ages with me,' he said. 'More or less. Few months older, in fact.'

'Thanks,' I laughed. 'That's good to know.'

'An older woman,' he said, raising his eyebrows.

For a moment it seemed we were flirting, almost. Then he asked me about the scar on my face and the moment dissolved with my too-brusque answer. He stood up to leave and I looked down at the laminate tabletop and the colours were loud and the day changed shape. I watched him walk through the swaying turbans of the waiters, watched him stoop his way out into the sunlight. As he pushed the door open he turned back, shrugged his shoulders and gave me a sad smile. The wire door swung shut. Instinctively, I put my hand to my face.

◎

Before bed that night as I moisturized my face, smoothing over the scar under my right eye, there was a knock at the door. I opened it and Arkay was there with a bunch of tuberose flowers tied with gold tinsel.

'I'm sorry. I didn't mean to upset you,' he said, handing me the flowers. The heavy musk scent flowed through the room. 'Really. I'm just out of practice. With women. I just want us to be friends.'

'Thank you,' I said. I put my hand on his shoulder. 'Thank you for saying that.'

'See you in the morning,' he said, stepping back. 'Sleep tight.'

◎

We spent days and evenings together after that. A fortnight wandering the bazaars of the pink city, absorbing the details of each other's lives. All the colours and shadings. Sometimes I'd catch him looking at me, a certain expression on his face.

Don't read too much into it, I said to myself.

One day he said to me, 'I've started dreaming about women.'

'Oh?'

'And I don't get it.' He shook his head. 'In the dream there's a woman touching a stone wall. Silver water pours onto the ground. In this dream, I'm saying to the woman, "I can't marry you. I'm a monk."'

'Sometimes I forget you're a monk,' I said, teasing him.

'Well.' He smiled, adjusted his robes and twisted the sandal-wood mala at his wrist. 'Aye. But I'm still a monk.' He smiled at me, held my gaze. 'Things just feel a bit, I don't know. Complicated. Just at the minute.'

'Life is always complicated.'

He looked at me, breathed deeply. 'What I mean is, since my mother died. These past months, it's all been different.'

'Of course.' I touched his arm, to reassure him. 'Grief changes everything.' Then I thought of my own mother and the sadness crashed down.

'Aye,' he said, moving his arm away. 'Everything.'

That night we took a taxi to the Rambagh Palace Hotel. We sat close in the back seat. Arkay had his arm around the edge of the seat behind me. He was dressed in what he called his civilian clothes – the loose khaki trousers, the white kurta. The stubble on his face was more pronounced. I thought he'd been drinking, but I couldn't be sure. I could hear the blue heat off his body and the energy between us.

We ordered Indian champagne. Surrounded by portraits of the last Maharajah shooting tigers dressed in pith helmet and jodhpurs. I insisted on paying. He drank quickly, while always seeming sober. It was something I'd noticed and it made me wonder. 'You drink a lot for a monk.' I tried to make a joke of it.

He shrugged and looked up at the portraits. 'Maybe.'

There was an awkward moment until one of the young waiters approached and we ordered a second bottle of champagne. When the waiter returned he looked at us absorbed in each other, sitting there. 'You are in love?' the waiter asked shyly.

We looked at each other, surprised by the question, and turned back to the boy in the bold turban. 'We are.' We said this at exactly the same time, laughing out loud, surprising ourselves even more.

'Only joking,' I said to Arkay and repeated it for the waiter. 'Only joking.'

The monk looked at me with an expression I couldn't read and took another sip of his drink. 'Aye,' he said to the waiter. 'Pals, that's all. *Good friends.*'

That night in the taxi, we kissed in the back seat, like teenagers. Tentative at first, then deeper. Back at the hotel we stumbled up the steps to my room, arms round each other, still laughing. Drunk.

When we got to my door he leant in close and said: 'What are you thinking?'

'I don't know, what are *you* thinking?'

'Not sure.' He stepped back. His eyes were large and sad. We embraced in the doorway and then he pulled away from me. 'Time I went,' he said. 'Should've gone hours ago.'

'You don't have to go.'

He shook his head. 'See you in the morning.'

'Sleep well,' I said. A dark hurt in my chest as he walked away.

I turned the key in the lock, walked into the room and threw myself on the bed. I used the remote to switch on the television and watched MTV for a while, trying to calm down. Everything pulsed in my body, as if all the colours inside me were changing. I lay there too sexed-up to sleep. I fantasized about fucking him in the taxi and came quickly. I lay there thinking about him for some time.

The next morning he knocked at the door inviting me for breakfast. He wore his monk's robes. His face was pale and his eyes a little bloodshot, a little wary. His hair wet and combed back. I kissed him on the mouth but he pushed me gently away.

'We have to talk,' he said. 'What happened last night? I could've gone to bed with you. I wanted to. Believe me. I started thinking: you and me. The two of us. The whole she-bang. But it's not real. You're my friend. There's my life in the monastery. You have your own life. Believe me, I'm sorry . . .'

'I'm not,' I said.

'We can be friends.'

'If that's how it has to be.'

'That's how it has to be,' he said. 'Friends?'

'OK,' I said. 'Friends.' The word fell cinder from my tongue.

'Sorted.' He smiled and steered me towards the door. 'Let's eat.'

We walked through the courtyard of the hotel. The

bougainvillea was dying from white to brown. There was a wooden ladder turned horizontally along the base of the hotel wall. There was the sound of digging in the garden, and a woman's pale voice floating out from a first-floor balcony. I looked at the ladder. I thought of how I could shape it, crop it, hang it on a wall. How it would look in a gallery space. I'd not thought about work for weeks, not since I left Bhopal, not since meeting him again.

We were quiet with each other and we were careful not to touch. We moved over to sit by the hotel pool. It was an ornamental pool full of marble lotus of different sizes and shapes. I ran a hand over the stone flowers, hearing the texture. The water, as in a real lotus pool, was muddy and shallow and still – a beautiful approximation. Arkay went to order breakfast. A kitchen-wallah walked past with silver sweets in his hand, touching fingers lightly with another man. I shot off a reel of photographs and promised to send them the prints. A wind passed over the circular pool and the leaves moved in a clockwise direction like a mantra or a wheel, like a pilgrim around a stupa. I had a headache. I felt I was slowly circling myself, trying to make sense of things.

I thought of my weight upon his thighs, how it would be, radiating heat to be near him.

Friends. Of course. It wasn't too late to step back. Nothing had happened. I tried to reason with myself: what I really wanted was a distraction. From the past, from my work. This must be what it was all about.

I looked again at the muddy water.

The monk walked along the stone path, interrupting my thoughts. 'I wanted to show you something.' He moved around to my left side. He took my arm and led me to where a peacock was displaying itself and fanning its tail, making a turquoise show against a low sandstone wall.

'What do you hear?' he asked.

'Red.'

'I keep telling you, how lucky.'

I pressed his hand, then let go. *This doesn't have to be difficult,* I tried to reassure myself. *This could be enough.*

We waited at Jaipur station. A dozen porters in orange and red turbans squatted at the edge of the platform waiting for customers; brass badges shone from their coat sleeves. Metal signs on the station wall showed various charges:

BY HEAD

BY WHEELBARROW

BY STRETCHER (2 OR 4 PERSONS) FOR THE

DISABLED

Half a dozen men in army fatigues and red epaulettes lifted a black metal trunk over the railway lines. An elderly woman in a pink sari carried a plastic basket, flashing brightly past the soldiers like a song. A young woman in a faded sari lifted a cup of chai to her lips. Her kohl-rimmed eyes startled over the rim of the cup. She was so beautiful that I went up and asked if I could take a photograph. Arkay was silent and withdrawn.

We had a compartment to ourselves; the floor was strewn with peanut shells. I was the lone woman in the carriage. The neighbouring compartments were full of men, their eyes hard upon me every time I moved. Arkay stared morosely out of the window or sat with his legs crossed, eyes shut, trying to meditate.

I couldn't get a grip on what was happening. Tension coiled in every gesture and conversation. We sat reading and his leg brushed against mine. I moved my leg away.

He looked up. 'We're not allowed to touch?'

Uncertain, I shifted back. Moments later, he moved away again.

The train from Jaipur to Jodhpur slipped past white cube houses with pale green doors. I marvelled at these desert towns of primary colours. The train slid past salt mounds and cracked salt flats. Past thatched huts and salmon-coloured earth. The train pushed on, out to the edges of the Thar Desert, sounding a plaintive horn through the saltflats and the brown knotted limbs of the khejri trees.

Some of the khejri trees had tiny green leaves. I focused on the angle of the branches, the sound and colour. 'It's the sacred tree of the Bishnoi people, one of the few plants to survive in the desert.' I read this out to Arkay from my guidebook, trying to engage him. 'They use the entire tree. The wood for ploughs. The leaves as fodder for camels and goats . . .' I looked up and he was staring out of the window.

He looked back at me, suddenly: 'I love that about you. That curiosity. I love it.'

This made me happier than I'd been in days. Then as soon as I became aware of it, I wanted to disrupt the feeling.

'What's wrong with you?' I said to him, and my tone was harsh. 'Are you feeling OK?'

'I'm OK.'

'You look terrible.' Although I was trying to provoke him, it was true. He looked smudged and unkempt. His eyes were bloodshot. He was losing weight.

'Worry about yourself,' he said. 'I'm fine.'

'You don't seem fine.'

'Just forget about it.'

I put the guidebook away and we sat in silence. I noticed the tin signs for Sonia Gandhi and the Congress Party as we neared Jodhpur. I saw the saffron BJP flags. I wanted to point all this out to him, to talk to him about it all, but he kept his eyes shut.

We stayed in separate rooms in a guest house with a view of the Mehrangarh Fort. The rooms had lemon walls, maroon ceiling fans and fuchsia shells along the ceiling. There were carved mahogany beds and pink marble flooring. The colours played discordantly. In India sometimes when I was tired, I longed for some grey. From the window I could see a rectangular well. Built for the Maharani in 1788, according to my guidebook. There was a small green shrine near the steps to the well. The water was now stagnant, buzzing with mosquitoes at dusk, but it still served as a place of worship. In the early evening women floated small candles on the water. I could hear a bruised sound as each candle lit up. Arkay walked down to the well and sat cross-legged on the steps. He gathered his robes about him and stared into the water for a long time. I took a photograph of him from my window.

From the balcony of the hotel I watched a bleached, tiny

squirrel sunning itself on a dirty wall. The squirrel then roused itself to hop and play among the blue-and-red Pepsi cartons. Brown goats scrabbled on the hill beneath the fort. Eagles circled the blue cube houses.

The desert air here was warmer and drier than in Jaipur. I felt tired from the proximity to what I wanted and what I couldn't have. There was a weight on my chest and a tightening around my throat. After this, my camera stayed in its case.

❁

In the foyer of the guest house I met a woman carrying a small urn. She was heading for Varanasi, she said. The urn contained the ashes of her pet dog and she planned to scatter these ashes over the River Ganges. Shortly after her dog died, she had conceived a much longed-for child. She was now five months pregnant and this child, she was certain, was the reincarnation of her beloved animal.

I told Arkay about the woman with the dog, the ashes in the urn, about her pilgrimage to Varanasi. 'I don't know,' I said. 'About the dog, about the baby . . .'

'Well.' He stood in the doorway tapping his foot. 'It's complex.'

I kept pushing. 'Can a dog *really* become a human being?'

'Can a human being become a mosquito?' he snapped. 'How the hell should I know?'

'But you're the monk . . .'

He shrugged. 'It's the Western linear view. It prevents you from seeing.'

'*My* Western linear view?'

'Maybe.'

'What kind of monk *are* you?'

'What do you want me to say?'

We stalked off to our separate hotel rooms. I cried long and hard about the gulf between us. At 2 a.m. there was a knock at the door. He stood there contrite and rumpled-looking; it was obvious he'd been drinking. 'Look,' he said. 'It wasn't anything. We both got upset. It was nothing. I'm still here. Your friend. Let me tell you about Varanasi . . .'

A sadhu walks up the steps of Manikarnika ghat carrying a metal pot. A monkey leaps from a rooftop above him.

Varanasi, Uttar Pradesh, 2001

ARKAY

We waited for the train. New Delhi station was crowded and hot. As we waited, I counted the signs that hung above the platform: Chief stationmaster, Commercial stationmaster, Assistant Commercial stationmaster. The ranks went on forever. Naga bought chai from a wheelbarrow stall. The chai came in terracotta cups then – now it's all plastic: in only a few years, the changes – and when we finished we ground the cups underfoot.

And I was flying almost, at the thought of this trip. Though not in the old way, not like that. It was more a kind of clarity, that's all I can tell you. And I tried to stay with it. Everything so clear, it seemed that through the train window there was too much happening. I had this often in India. *Too much happening.* I hadn't touched a drop, not since Kerala, and the world was still bright and shiny and painful. Maybe the world was always this way.

I sighed. Naga looked up and I said, 'Just thinking of Kerala.'
He smiled and turned back to his book. 'It was good for you.'
'Aye.'

We sat at opposite ends of the couchette, legs drawn up, reading. I took off my sandals, flexed my dusty feet. Naga took off his shoes but kept his socks on. I'd never seen Naga in sandals or barefoot. He was absorbed in his book and I studied his face: his smooth round face with the long earlobes, *Buddha ears* – for the first time I really saw this and I told him, and he laughed. I always got a kick out of making him laugh.

I breathed in and breathed out, focusing on the exhalation. I looked out of the window. In the distance there was a man in a grey kurta and grey trousers taking red bricks from a bullock cart. The man and the bullock kept adjusting their postures, moving to each other's tempo. Naga also looked out, fascinated. 'Yes,' he said, smiling wide, 'they are old friends.' The marks on his face stretched tight across his cheekbones when he smiled. The train stopped in the middle of the tracks and we watched them for a long time till we moved off.

Naga had been to Varanasi several times before. We planned to spend a few days and then go on to Bodh Gaya for teachings with the Dalai Lama. The other monks from Dharamsala had gone on ahead. Before the trip I was maybe – what's the old word? *Feart*. How would it be with the bodies and the flames? How would it be, because Lama was very ill, maybe dying, and I didn't want to leave him. Lama had become steadily weaker. 'My heart's not good,' he said. 'I'm old, I'm tired. I'm ready.' This stirred up all the selfish lonely thoughts: *When Lama dies – then what?* Many times I could've packed and left the monastery. Over the years I'd been tempted. But Lama kept me steady. He was my first teacher; he'd kept me on my path.

But he urged us to go and said how important it was, once in a lifetime at least, to get to Benares. 'Go,' he said in English. He waved us off with one of his favourite Tibetan expressions: 'Don't enjoy sadly.'

I sighed, my meditation disrupted, my book in my lap. Naga seemed to read my mind and leant over pointing to my heart centre. 'The teacher is always inside.' Then he gestured out the window. 'The teacher is everywhere.'

'Aye,' I said. 'You're right. Course you are.'

❁

When we got to Varanasi we stayed in the newer part of town, in an apartment on the top floor of a cinema complex. The manager was a retired army officer – Major Joshi, the brother of a monk from Dharamsala. He'd fought in Bangladesh, he told us. He'd fought in Kashmir. He'd fought on the Chinese border. He was a big, proud, good-looking man with a smooth brown face and white hair. He walked quickly, his barrel chest pushed out. He was surrounded at all times by a dozen people who fell into step. He ran the cinema like a barracks. We could see any film for free, he said, as guests of his establishment. The first film was a blockbuster and it lasted four hours. I didn't understand much and Naga translated the best bits. We sat in the crowded noisy cinema while all around us people ate and talked: *What an excellent film this is.*

After the film we took a trip to the ghats. 'There's someone we must meet,' said Naga. The Major's driver took us into the old town on a motorbike, the three of us stacked up on the seat, the suspension straining under the weight. We spun through the tiny alleyways of the old town to the edge of the ghats. From there we walked to to the river and down to Manikarnika Ghat.

The buildings were grimed and manky from the smoke. Small monkeys hopped from balcony to balcony. There was a background hum of chanting. The river was full of marigolds, plastic bags, detergent bottles and charcoal. It was minging. Barge loads full of wood floated down the Ganges from Bihar. The boatmen flew tiny kites across the sky as they waited for punters.

I felt as if I flowed with the river. Flowed with my life for the first time.

A beggar woman in grey cloth sat by the side of the river. Her head was shaved. A widow, said Naga, and told me her story. It was an all-too-common story, he said. She was one of thousands of widows left by the Ganges each year. Conned by sons and sons-in-law to visit the Holy City at least once in a lifetime. Even if she knew her fate in advance – and who can ever know for certain? – even if she knew, she would follow the son because there was no choice when a family was poor and a widow was a burden. She would wake up one or maybe two days after and the family would be gone. She'd be left in one of the small rooms in the old city to wear white, to bow her shaved head, to offer prayers in one of the widows' hostels or to end her days begging out along the river. There were rumours that the same men who paid for prayers also paid for use of the women, especially the younger ones. An old, old story, said Naga. The old widow in her grey robes had seen it all. She shuffled up to firangis loading their cameras. There was the familiar gesture: the cupped hand around the upturned bowl, the movement from hand to mouth. Most turned away. It was hard not to turn away.

We kept walking until we came to a small Hindu temple. 'Wait here,' said Naga. He came out some minutes later with an old sadhu in lime and gold cloth, a mala around his neck, an

aluminium pot tied to his hip. He had long white hair and a saffron tikka on his forehead. Naga helped him climb up the steps.
Naga said, 'This is my first teacher.' The sadhu greeted me with
a big smile; his small bright eyes took in everything. After a life
of meditation and teaching he'd left it all and now lived as a true
ascetic in this temple to Shiva. The old sadhu nodded as Naga
told his story. No one knew his past, Naga said, how gifted a
master, a Buddhist monk with a great knowledge of Sanskrit.
The sadhu shook his head, tried to protest, but Naga continued.
'The people here see something special,' he said. 'Always, there
is food in his alms bowl, always water to drink. But if you leave
anything more, he always gives it away.'

We followed the sadhu. 'Now,' he said. 'Now we must practise.' We sat up all night and watched the burning bodies. I
clocked each change in colour and texture of the skin, the way
the fluids ran, all of it. I struggled, it'd be a lie to say any different. All through the night we watched one body in particular,
that of an old man. We meditated on the changes as his body
bent in the flames with the chanting all around. As dawn broke,
the sadhu told us to meditate on our own deaths. The timing
of which was uncertain, he said. All that was certain was that it
would come.

After dawn we returned to the apartment. I was knackered and
yet strangely wired after the night on the ghats. The Major
saluted us as we climbed the stairs up past the projection booth.
Inside the apartment the Major's houseboy made chai. We sat in
meditation as the scent of cardamon pods, ginger and cloves

drifted through from the saucepan in the kitchen. I thanked Naga for the introduction to his teacher. Naga smiled, his knees creaked as he got up. He took his chai and walked slowly to his room. 'No need to thank me,' he said.

'I mean for everything. You know that.'

He put his hands up in namaste. 'Sleep well,' he said, turning to his room. He left his shoes outside the door and I saw the cotton packing, bloodied at the toes.

On our last day in Varanasi we got a rickshaw to Sarnath, the site of the Buddha's first sermon. We stood a long time in front of the statues of the Buddha and his disciples in the deer park. Naga picked up some leaves fallen from a Bodhi tree and we kept them for Lama.

'I am old. I am tired.' Lama's voice was in my head as we travelled back. There was the feel of rain in the air. The skies changed, turned dark and erupted into an electrical storm. We took it as a sign. When we got to the next monastery we heard the news of Lama's death. And I was calm when the news hit – how they'd taken Lama to a hospital in Delhi and he'd died on the operating table. I repeated it to myself, to make it real. *My guru is dead*. But I couldn't seem to take it in. Naga and I got off the train in Delhi and went straight to the hospital. We sat in vigil with Lama's body in a small room off the main corridor. At the moment of death, the doctors said that Lama had sat upright in meditation. They pushed the body back down. Again he sat up. The doctors had never seen anything like it.

Lama's heart centre stayed warm for three days. The body

didn't start to decompose although the days were hot. Then on the fourth day it was clear he was gone. Naga said, 'Be happy. He's succeeded into death.'

My guru is dead. It finally hit me. And inside there was this great hollow feeling. I saw how it'd run, my life to this point. *Trust nae fucker.* This had been my father's mantra. In the village when I was growing up, this was how it was. But Lama had shown me a different path and another way of being in the world.

At Lama's cremation I saw letters and symbols smoke up from the fire.

'Look,' I said to Naga. 'The signs. Lama's next incarnation.'

'I didn't see,' said Naga.

'Look,' I insisted, pointing to the outlines. 'A dholak drum. The figure of a man – or maybe a woman? Flower shapes . . .'

'Maybe,' said Naga. He looked at me with a frown.

'I could go . . .'

He put his hand on my arm. 'Stay. Be still. Accept. Already, you are trying to run.'

My guru was dead. The night of the cremation he appeared in a dream. 'Follow my ash prints,' he said. 'One day you will find me. I will not be what you expect.'

A young boy puts his hand into a hole in the ground.
Nearby are fragments of bone and the shadow of a
camel.

Jodhpur, Rajasthan, September 2004

FRANÇOISE

We kept talking right through the night. 'And so,' I said to him. 'Did you go looking?'

'For Lama? For his incarnation? No. I'm still waiting. When the time comes I'll know. But Naga was right.'

'About what?'

'I grasped at the signs. I thought the signs or the search could save me . . .'

'Save you?'

'From grief. Loneliness. God only knows. Without your teacher it can feel lonely, this path . . .'

'You don't have to feel lonely,' I said, reaching out to put my hand on his arm.

He didn't move away. He moved closer. And then it happened. We slept together for the first time and all the tension between us, all the dance of it, all the frustration and desire momentarily dissolved. The pattern was set: we had sex and argued and reconciled and fell apart all the way through Rajasthan. He drank even more heavily and the weight fell off him.

'What is it with the drinking?' I confronted him one night. 'I don't get it. Aren't you happy here? With me? Isn't this enough?'

'Maybe I'm too happy,' he said, trying to make a joke of it. 'Worry about yourself.'

We argued usually after he'd been drinking and we'd spent a good day together. As if he had to disrupt the calm somehow; couldn't quite trust it. I was pulled in different directions. Wanting and not wanting him. It took all my energy.

One night I said, 'You argue to create a barrier . . .'

'Spare me the fucking pop psychology,' he said as he pushed past me out into the night and down to the liquor stall at the end of the street.

❁

There were good days and bad days and I was hooked in. Then he began to stay out all night, returning so drunk that he'd piss in the corner of the room or piss in our bed, like a child. I'd wake in the morning and wash the sheets in the handbasin or the bath and neither of us could say a word.

It wasn't always like this. There were times when we were close and happy. Times when we didn't push each other away.

'What about the monastery?'

He raised a glass: 'Who said I'm going back?'

'The sabbatical?'

'I can extend it.'

'Do they know you're here with me?'

He didn't answer. 'You worry too much,' he said. 'One day at a time.' And he'd hold me and tell me he loved me.

'You don't love me?' he'd ask, seeing the look on my face.

'It's not that.'

'What, then?'

I couldn't answer him. I couldn't explain it to myself. Instead, I'd open a sketchbook and pick up a pencil, start drawing.

'You could've been a Zen master.' His voice was heavy. 'Really, with that focus,' he continued. 'A Zen master.'

'But I'm not.' I put down the pencil. 'I'm really not.'

'What's wrong? What is it?'

'I can't be all that to you, the life you've left behind.'

He pulled me close. 'I'm not looking for a replacement.'

Sometimes, we could allow ourselves to be happy.

We came to a sort of truce. We moved on to Jaisalmer, a short overnight trip from Jodhpur. We arrived before dawn along with four other tourists and the drivers met us draped in huge blankets to ward off the cold. They left us at the edge of the walled city and we walked up to find a hotel. We shared a sky-blue room at the Hotel Paradise.

In the morning sunshine Jaisalmer shone gold and I began to feel better. Maybe he'd get over this. Maybe it was a phase. An adjustment to a new life, to this relationship. *Take it as it comes*, I told myself. Below the ramparts of the Hotel Paradise pigeons sat in latticed porticos making a dull full-throated sound. Young boys played cricket in bare feet, arguing and shouting. A squadron of RSS boys marched in formation around a patch of dry earth. They wore saffron scarves and khaki uniforms. They marched for hours in the hot sun, gripping their lathis and kicking up dust.

'Like Hitler Youth,' I said to Arkay.

'Aye,' he said. 'The prototype. Anti-Muslim, Hindu

Nationalist. Their BJP pals lost the election, though. That has to be a good thing.'

'But this Hindutva stuff won't just go away.'

'Depends on who inflames it. Congress won by not inflaming . . .'

'Will Sonia be President?'

'Who knows? The big question. Not even Congress knows.'

We spent the day wandering the narrow lanes of the city. We took a rickshaw to the cenotaphs on the outskirts of Jaisalmer to watch the sunset. We paused in front of tiny headstones – some with male, some with female figures. In the distance, black crows wheeled around the fort.

Other tourists arrived. We were surrounded by a Korean tour group in leather cowboy hats and small bibles tucked into their shirt pockets; bandannas wound around mouths and noses.

He nudged me: 'A good look.'

I laughed, and we were happy with each other in that moment. I realized I was waiting for these moments, holding out for them. Then the anxiety would rise up, waiting for the wheel to turn; straining to hear how it would go between us.

In the middle distance a beggar boy moved forward on his hands. He had one withered leg and a stump for the other. He covered ground quickly in a crab-like motion, trying to get to the tourists before we drifted into taxis and cycle rickshaws. The sun burnt down in its own aureole of gold, pink and white. A melancholy sound like a piano scale. I could have framed it like that but I put down my camera, content just to listen.

The next day we resisted all efforts by the hotel owner to make us join a camel trek. Instead we took an auto-rickshaw sixteen kilometres out of town. The driver took us to the Jain temples.

I had my period and, mindful of tradition, urged Arkay to go in without me. I waited for him outside. I was relieved to have the time alone, sitting in the shade of a neem tree. How did this happen? I asked myself. How did I let myself get so drawn in with this person, so drawn under? The neem tree was charred and knotted like driftwood, like the remains of a shipwreck. I thought how I'd like to use this tree. Small donkeys nuzzled each other, rolling over and over in the dust. Two camels lay resting beneath their humps. I noticed a broken leather sandal tangled in a green hessian bag. I took a photograph. I shot off a reel. Nearby were fragments of pale jawbone and teeth. A goat, maybe. For the first time in weeks I made notes in my workbook. I picked up one of the bone fragments and held it to my ear, like a shell.

Three drivers lay in the shade while their passengers walked the site. The drivers were young and slightly built. Filmi music blared from a portable radio. I took a photograph of them against the trees. One of the drivers walked over to me, switching briefly to English, gesturing at the bone fragments on the ground. 'In monsoon-time,' he said, 'everything is underwater. When the water goes, small flowers come and then die. The bones of dead animals come up. Old buildings stand again.'

Huge holes studded the ground. 'King cobra,' the driver said. One of the boys put his hand into the cobra hole and just as quickly withdrew it. He looked around for a response with a gap-toothed grin. I applauded him. 'Bravo,' I said. I picked up my camera and he obliged, again putting his hand into the deep hole. The other drivers pushed and shoved and showed off for my benefit.

Out beyond the Jain temples, windmill generators and oil wells marked the landscape. An Indian fighter jet flew low overhead towards Pakistan.

The deserts of Rajasthan. That trip with Arkay. The sandflows of the desert arced and curved inside me and a sudden pink wind, a desert squall, rose up as I sat there.

A column of dust and light, a ghost wind – a butaria, that's what the driver called it.

A monk walks away from the camera. Shadows fall across his back.

Jaisalmer, Rajasthan, September 2004

ARKAY

It happened like this: I met Fran again and we slept together. Got used to each other and it was good. All of it new. I stayed on sabbatical with no real thoughts for the future. After a decade of discipline and practice there were no more routines and I was high as the past slid from me. I no longer meditated. There was no need. I was drinking again, just socially mind, just with her. Her touch made me happy, my nerve ends on fire. I felt lucky. At first, it was like this. I loved her so much, it was painful.

I loved her so much I had to push her away.

Fuck knows, it started in Jodhpur. Everything so intense, one minute it's night and the next it was dawn and I'd crawl into bed; fold myself in. Late afternoon, some kind of grip as if words were stuck. And who knew why this should be happening when – let's face it – I was happy, happier than I'd ever been, but the hammering in my chest and the lock shut round my throat and then I was back in the village, the same feeling, sat in my room when I've had a good day and I'm staring out the window tensing for my father and then his voice and everything starts to slide and the good day turns into something very different and next I know, I'm walking out our hotel room, 'Won't be long.' This is how it started and at first she believes me, and I believe myself and I walk down the narrow streets, past the

blue-wash houses and up a lane to a place I'd seen on the way
to the Fort. Clocked it and filed it away. A hole-in-the-wall
with the hard core outside: thin unshaved men, mad-eyed like
cartoon jakeys – just like the Grassmarket – and they're drinking Lady Di gin and Princess vodka and I nod as I go past,
smile – tell myself I'm just looking – past the grille on the
window and the rows of dusty bottles and I wonder how long
they've sat there, those bottles – and just the thought of going
in, maybe walking back, pushing through the turnstile and into
the fluorescent – just the thought of it starts to take the edge off
and I think, what the fuck, as the old boys make way and the
turnstile creaks as I push through – and I'm smiling now and if
I were still a whistler, I'd be whistling, and I'm more calm than
I've been for hours as I blow dust off the bottles and think about
what to get. I've no choice, really, and so it's the Lady Di and
a few Cobras. I've been good. I deserve it. I'm happy as. The
tight feeling goes as I manoeuvre it all up onto the counter and
pull the rupees out my pocket, look up at the framed photos of
Gandhi and Nehru and the clink of bottles – that sedative
sound – already I'm feeling better, almost one hundred per cent
and then I'm out, past the old boys, and I loose the cap on the
gin, close my eyes and the edges are smoothed, no doubt about
it, those sharp places inside. And I think I'll stay for a bit, she
couldn't mind – a half an hour, maybe, no more than that. One
of the old boys sees my orange T-shirt and shaved head.
'Bhagwan?' And I laugh, like a nutter. 'No, not the Bhagwan.
I've no interest in a fucker with his bodyguards and Mercedes.
Stealing from Buddha and Jesus and God knows where.' And I
tell them I'm a monk, or was, till very recent. And we stand
tamping our feet for the nights are cold in these desert towns

but I can't speak their language and they can't speak mine so I shake my head again, 'No, not the Bhagwan,' and swallow some more. Then an old man starts to dance with the bottle held high. And who knows how long we're sat there, watching?

Some velvet morning when I'm straight.

There was that line, a deep pulse in my head. An old tune and a man's voice – spoken more than sung. Then it comes, the image almost comic – Lee Hazlewood in an Afghan coat. That line kept playing to me all through our time together. I'd start humming it inside myself. I'd remember every sound and taste and touch before I got this way. Everything up until the last drink.

It was all hammering regret in the morning because it got to be a pattern and she said I needed help and I couldn't explain to her or to myself what I needed, but it kept on somehow. 'What are you afraid of?' she wanted to know. 'Just tell me, and I'll try to help.'

'It can't last,' I said to her. My self-fulfilling prophecy.

She loves me.

My mind blew apart like a daisy chain, like a child's rhyme, beating hard. Because if she could see me, really see me, all the shite inside?

She loves me not.

FRANÇOISE

The train moved slowly and the passage of time smelt of something long gone. Two boys in white kurtas and pink caps rode bicycles along the train tracks. Women and children walked beside the rails, balancing shawl-wrapped bundles on their heads. A tall lithe man folded sheets at the edge of a rail platform. His long dark arms folded first one way and then another. Three palm trees formed a trident shape beyond that. It seemed to me that you could enter at any point into this and merge with it. A woman swathed in heat and mint-green fabric shimmered in the distance, one arm steadying a basket on her head, the other arm down and her gold bracelets glinting against her skin.

I sat by myself in a train carriage strewn with peanut shells. I steadied the camera at the window. Everything ached.

I loved him. But it wasn't enough. With the drink, the way he was, and the dreams. Always the same dreams, the *speedy* dreams: boys from his childhood, men from the village, the hard men, the drinkers, Dan Tierney, they'd all pursue him. He could never escape and never fight back in the dreams, he said.

I'd wanted to look after him. Some people affect you like that. The worse it got, the harder I tried.

When we first got together I'd sit and look at him: his large grey eyes shone and his hair sparked copper in the light. I remember wanting to capture it. Maybe something with fire, it came to me. I'd make a flame portrait. Use a bronze filter. Or maybe a Polaroid. Mess with it, mark the surface. Soak it and leave it to warm in the sun. I told him all this and he looked puzzled for a moment. Raised his glass, angled his good side towards me.

'A blame portrait?'

'No.' I laughed. 'Flame,' I repeated. 'A flame portrait.'

He drained the glass. 'Seems about right.'

I never did take that photograph. I kept travelling through Rajasthan, aimless and alone. I went on to Udaipur and took photos at the dry edge of the lake. I tried oblique views of the Palace. Tried to hear things differently. But every shot was bad and I knew it. I'd wake up clumsy and heavy. This went on for weeks. *You've been a leaver all your life*, I tried to reassure myself. *This, too, will pass.* Tried to talk myself around. *Be patient. Breathe.*

I wrote to Aruna and told her I'd be coming back through Delhi. From there I planned to return to Bhopal, but I began to feel unwell. Exhausted. Some kind of infection, I was sure of it. I rang Shahid and he said, 'Rest. Go to the doctor. The project can wait.'

I wrote to Naga. I gave him Aruna's telephone number. I told him he could contact me there. I told him that if he saw Arkay not to give him my address.

In the guest house in Udaipur the waiter called after me. 'Madam,' he called, and I could hear footsteps as he ran to catch up. 'Madam, your bags!'

All my life I'd packed quickly and left quickly. My camera bags were always the first and last things I checked. Now I moved as if trawling through mud. With the work I could always cut or crop or frame things somehow. I could understand the fragment as the whole. But in everyday life you had to endure things just as they happened. It was so difficult to sense the whole from its parts.

In a shutter-click of time how a person can affect you.

I could have stayed. It would've been easy to stay because I loved him and was heart-sore and no longer so young. But I knew that if I'd stayed with him I would have gone under. Would have never come up.

ARKAY

She was the woman of my life. I know that now. And I understood that she was complicated, that she knew what love was, really. I couldn't ever match up, that's the truth of it. That's the thing about women and men. Women can give and give and give. Sometimes it makes you want to hurt them. Not physically. But you know you're afraid of giving like that even when you want to. Even if you could.

I knew fuck-all about intimacy after all that time. I was unprepared and I'd been so sure on my path. Too sure perhaps. A little doubt is good, Naga always used to say. I've got many reasons and too many excuses. She had her work and she seemed more complete than I could ever hope to be. Maybe I envied her that. Perhaps I worried that after a time she'd have no need of me.

We travelled through Rajasthan. Wonderful, sad, difficult months. There was one night in the beginning, before we got it together, that I'd lost all appetite. I lay on the bed thinking of her. Thinking of her a lot. I'd not been like that about a woman, not really, for a long long time. After the first few years it all got easier. The routine of watching the mind and working with it. Observing it rise and fall. But after all that time, *she* got to me. The scent of her. The way she laughed. What you saw with her was what you got.

I'd been on the way down after the time in Scotland. After my mother. Can I say it was bad timing? Needing someone to ease the fall?

Straight off, I was in love with Fran. All the classic signs and symptoms.

Just couldn't admit it.

◌

It took us three months. By then, we both knew it wasn't working. 'I'm a jakey,' I told her when it got too much. She nodded, not really believing. Not wanting to believe. She didn't understand just how bad it could get. She thought she could save me.

Isn't that what women think?

And I wanted salvation. God knows. That's all I ever wanted.

We travelled. We made plans. In each place, things got worse. She'd rinse the sheets, hang them out on the balcony of each room we stayed in, and then I'd insist we move on. Avoid the cleaners and the hotel owners. To avoid answers.

Each time I'd wake up, curled up, frozen. *This is happening, again?* Fran would smooth it over. The afternoons and early evenings were the best. We were together and it was enough. I wanted it to continue; never wanted it to stop. 'One more couldn't hurt,' I'd say. And because she loved me, at first she kept me company. Nothing hurt with one more drink on a long holiday with someone you love. Nothing hurt as long as we kept moving.

I could've gone to her and said: 'I'm not ready for this.' But I didn't have the words to say exactly what I wanted or what I feared. It seems clear to me now. Happiness exists so you take it for granted, fuck it up. Know it only when it's spent.

It got bad by the end of three months. Nearly every night was bad. She started to keep count of the bottles. Started to plead with me. 'Don't you think you've had enough?'

One is too many. One is never enough.

Inside myself, the old cliché. I turned her into a banshee in my mind. She became a voice: nagging, insistent. The arguments got worse. I was always contrite in the morning.

After three months she was gone. And I lay there, clutching my little-boy sheets for comfort.

RETURN

Two empty camera bags lie open on the ground. A taxi driver leans down towards the bags. A woman's reflection is caught in the back window.

New Delhi, November 2004

FRANÇOISE

When I arrived in Delhi it was after midnight and the house was quiet. Surjit and Aruna were sleeping and Jigme opened the door. He helped me carry the luggage upstairs. My back ached, everything ached. I found comfort in the familiar dark furniture and the portraits in the hallway. I eased into this house again with the scent of incense as I went up to the room.

I came down to a late breakfast and they were waiting for me as if I'd never been away. Surjit took my right hand and brought it to his lips in one of his elaborate old-fashioned gestures. Aruna hugged me tight. 'You're back,' she said. 'But so thin! You're not well . . .'

'Stomach?' Surjit interjected. 'With foreigners, it's always the stomach.'

'Must be,' I said. I had no energy to put up an argument.

We talked about Rajasthan and about the train journey. We discussed the new houseboy and what I wanted to eat for breakfast. We spoke about Sonam.

'You found him?' Aruna clasped her hands. 'But this is wonderful!'

'Yes.'

'And? His health? His family?' She was full of questions.

'He's well. He thanks you for the money. For remembering him.'

Then I told them the whole story.

Aruna sat quietly, taking it all in. Surjit leant back in his chair. 'Who would have thought?' He raised his eyebrows. 'The angry boy would become a monk?'

'People change,' said Aruna. 'Life changes us.'

'My wife is an eternal optimist.'

'He saved us, Surjit. It's your pride, only. You've never forgotten. You've never forgiven yourself.'

Surjit muttered something and took a sip of water. Then he shook out the newspaper, ignoring his wife. 'What do you think of the election result?' He turned to me but didn't wait for an answer. Manmohan Singh had become India's first Sikh Prime Minister but Surjit was not pleased. He started to read sections of the paper out loud. An article about the ongoing conflict over the Ayodha mosque. 'Manmohan Singh!' Surjit shook his head. 'Too soft on the Muslims. For centuries, the Muslims invade and destroy. Hindus knock down one mosque in Ayodhya. A mosque built on the birthplace of Lord Ram. And now these Muslims. So extreme!'

I drank my chai and tried to ignore the churning in my stomach. 'But from what I've read . . .'

'I have Muslim friends,' he interrupted, 'and I would help them because they are my friends. But I have no time for their religion.'

I swallowed hard. 'But all religions have extremists.'

'Have *you* ever suffered at *their* hands?' Surjit raised his voice.

'No,' I had to admit. 'No, I haven't.'

Surjit spread his arms wide, lowered his tone and seemed almost indulgent. 'My dear, that is exactly *why* you can talk like this.'

I shifted in my seat and rearranged the fruit on my plate. 'I'm just trying to understand, Surjit. I know you've lived through . . .'

He looked over the top of his glasses, held his hand up and said not unkindly: 'I've lived through things you could *never* understand. Things you couldn't possibly imagine.'

Aruna arranged a late appointment for me with Dr Chatterjee, one of her clients. I told the doctor my symptoms and how I was sure it was an infection. She asked me how long I'd been ill. Then she asked me about my last bleeding, the monthly cycle, how regular it was? She wrote everything down and then asked me directly: 'Maybe, you are pregnant?'

I sat up straight. 'No, that's not possible.' I was adamant.

'You are sure?'

'Yes. Well . . . yes . . . we always used . . .'

She leant forward. 'Always?'

'Well, only one time that I can remember . . . one time maybe . . . towards the end.'

She looked at her desk calendar and picked up a pencil. 'When?'

I thought back. 'Over two months ago,' I said to her. 'I guess, around then.'

'I see.' She reached into her drawer and pulled out a box. She gave me instructions and I went to the bathroom. Ten minutes later she called to me across the crowded room and I stepped over a young boy with his leg in a brace and went into the office again.

'It's true,' she said. 'Just as I thought.'

I sat there for a moment not looking at her, as if I hadn't heard. I focused instead on the eye chart above her chair, tracing the sounds and colours, fixating on the letters. I said, 'Are you sure?'

'Positive.'

I started shaking and then she got up quickly and walked around from her desk. I was crying hard and she put an arm around me. 'In Delhi there are many clinics,' she said, trying to reassure me. 'Many clinics. But there's little time.' She glanced at the calendar again. 'Big decisions.' She smoothed my hair back from my face.

'Please don't worry,' she soothed. 'Please don't worry.'

I told Aruna everything and begged her not to tell Surjit.

'What will you do?'

'There are clinics, the doctor said.'

'Clinics?' Her tone was disapproving. 'You are no longer so young.'

'But . . .'

'This may be your last chance.'

'Aruna, I never . . .'

'This, I do not understand. Every woman wants a child.'

'Not every woman.'

'Take your time,' she urged. 'Think about it. In any case, you should tell him.'

'Arkay?'

'Yes.'

'Why?'

'Because he's the father.'

'It's not a good idea.'

'Françoise. He's still the father.' She looked at me hard. 'You *could* be a mother.'

'But I don't want to be.'

'What are you afraid of?'

I looked over at the portrait of Aruna as a young bride. 'Isn't everyone afraid?'

I thought back to the mothers of my youth. Each generation believes themselves to be different. Such confidence: *I will not make the same mistakes.* Motherhood was a vocation, that's what the nuns used to say. But what kind of vocation? I used to ask. I only knew how the imaginaton cried out like a child in the night. I had to get up, follow it and answer that cry. What would happen with an actual child? Wouldn't I end up hollowed out, unable to dream, unable to create?

'Maybe I'll send him a letter,' I said to Aruna. 'But a child won't make things right.'

'You don't know.'

'It's gone beyond that.'

'Things change.'

'Aruna, you have to understand. Believe me. A child won't fix things.'

'Slow down,' Aruna comforted. She passed me chai, listened quietly. 'There's still time,' she said, 'still time.'

ARKAY

I got the bus to Dharamsala and a lift from there. The familiar
row of white stupas shone in the headlights. There were monks
in frieze positions all along the path. In maroon robes they
paced or sat with texts in hand. Some chanted. There were
cubes of light from small rooms. Young monks stood on the balcony watching my arrival.

It was the moment I'd looked forward to. Naga would know
what to do. Naga would help me with this. Yet the closer I came
to seeing him again the slower I walked, more and more uncertain.
As soon as I entered the monastery there was the familiar scent of
sandalwood and I dropped my bag on the ground and Naga was
there to greet me, full of enthusiasm. Then he saw the look on my
face. 'My friend. What is it? What is wrong with you?'

'A long story,' I said as we walked through the monastery.

'You must tell me.'

'Not now. I'm knackered.'

Naga was hurt by my tone. 'Rest,' he said. 'Rest. Have chai
now. Sit.' He opened the door to his room and it all pressed
in on me, this life I had left. I clocked the single futon on the
wood platform. There was a stool, a small table. A candle and
a box of matches. A bright thangka hung on one wall. A set of
robes were neat on a hanger. The one alms bowl on a shelf. I

had to remind myself of this pared-down other life.

'Sit,' Naga repeated.

'I'll wash first.' I relaxed a little. 'Then we can talk.' I unpacked clean robes then walked the length of the corridor to the shower room. I slid the rusty latch and sat on a plastic stool with the bucket of water filling slow from the tap. I grasped the small plastic saucepan, dipped it into the bucket. I soaped and lathered myself. Again I filled the bucket, poured the warm water over. Then I leant back against the rough brick wall and closed my eyes.

The warm water calmed me. I dried off and opened the door. I'd forget about Françoise; I told myself this was possible. Things couldn't come undone so easily. *Try to meditate on the difficult thing,* I told myself. *The obstacle is your friend.* I could go back, a new man to this old life. I was sure of it.

❁

Naga ordered chai from the kitchen. As I came out of the shower room dressed in clean robes I saw a young monk knock three times at Naga's door and hand over the tray. I followed in behind him and sat on a floor cushion.

Naga started to speak. 'My friend . . .'

'I met someone.'

'Ah . . .'

'A woman . . .'

'Hahn . . .'

'But it's over.'

Naga frowned. 'And now?'

'I'm not sure,' I said. I put my head in my hands.

We sat in silence. Naga passed me a cup, poured the tea and

I studied the thangka on the opposite wall.

'It didn't work out,' I said.

Naga looked down at the floor, adjusted his robes.

'It was Fran.'

He sat back as if I'd hit him. 'Françoise?'

'Aye.' I smiled, tried to make light of it. 'And you, mind, it was you that introduced us in the first place.'

◊

I waited. I tried hard, for sure, to see if I missed her any less. I was off the drink. Back in my old life back on the straight and narrow, but I dreamt of her constantly.

She holds my prick and touches me and reaches into and through me. My robes clatter to the ground.

Spun out by the dreams, I confided in the Abbot. Spilled the whole sorry tale and he listened, sat back, closed his eyes. When I was done he told me only to be mindful, to acknowledge the thoughts. 'Allow them to come up,' he said, 'allow them to go. Meditate on this: closeness without possession.' I struggled hard.

I said to Naga, 'I'm too attached to her, I'm sliding. I have no peace.'

I looked in the mirror and couldn't recognize myself any more with the weight falling off. For a while now I'd had trouble. A pain under the ribs. Knackered all the time but not only that. Just couldn't keep a lid on things. Kept thinking about my mother, my past, and it all came back in Technicolor. I got thinking of my father and his life. His drinking and where it led him. What it had meant for us.

The drink.

Desire for Fran brought up all the old stuff. Not that I was on the drink any more, not here, but I wanted to, that was the truth of it. Ever since I came back. Nights were the worst. There was a pressing on my lungs and it was hard to breathe. I sweated and shivered.

'Maybe a retreat?' Naga suggested. I grasped at the idea as if it would save me. As if it would truly get me back what I'd lost.

At 6 a.m. the sound of the gong echoed down the mountain. Before dawn we went to the dining room for chai. Everyone was quiet and the morning was clear and cool as we made our way to the Gompa. It was a general retreat at a monastery nearby. Open to the public. The place was full of Westerners.

I sat in my robes with a striped Nepali blanket over my shoulders. I settled into position; shifted on my sit-bones, levelled my knees. I inhaled deeply and when I breathed it hurt. For months it'd hurt and I'd pushed it away. My hands shook as I placed them palms up, forefinger and thumb together.

The microphone clicked on. 'Gather yourself,' said Naga. 'It's so busy, this life of speed and aggression. Gather yourself. Bring your mind back home.' He dedicated the session to all sentient beings. My mind wandered first to a cold bottle of Kingfisher, then to breakfast, to the steaming semolina porridge, a cup of hot . . . then Fran's face . . . the scar under her eye . . . I tried to bring my mind back . . . focus on the cool of the inhalation . . . a monkey clattered over the tin roof . . . the warmth of the exhalation . . . the English boy to my right coughed . . . the Israeli man behind cleared his throat . . . the Danish girl in front uncrossed her legs, her knees clicked . . . I opened my eyes . . . she was gorgeous . . . closed my eyes . . . a feeling, unbearable, like pins and needles spread across my chest and down my legs. I wanted to get up, to walk away. At the top of Macleod Gange near the taxi stand there was a stall, if I could maybe . . . Naga said: 'When the mind wanders, name the thoughts, don't follow. Pick the mind up and place it down.' I saw my mother's face, struggled with an urge to weep . . . pick the mind up and place it . . . name the thought . . . Lama, with the bells on his feet. . . maybe now was the time? His next incarnation? The generator started . . . a dog barked . . . breathe . . . maybe I'd walk down the hill past the plastic bags snagged in trees, past the huge red monkeys. Then Naga spoke again: 'So often in life we have a longing,' he said, as if speaking directly to me. 'But it's our-selves we long for, a peace inside.' He dedicated the session the same as he started it, for all beings. I opened my eyes. My right leg cramped. I shifted my sit-bones on the cushion, rotated my ankles, slowly stood up. Bright early light slanted across the room, catch-ing the gold upturned palms of the Buddha.

As I stood up, I had a sudden flash of myself in a new life. I'd go looking for Lama. I'd have Fran by my side. I could make everything right. I could try. It was worth a shot. Again, I wanted to run. *Slow down,* I said to myself. *Take it easy.* As Naga made final prostrations before the Buddhas, I saw the heels of his brown socks were almost worn through.

The rest of the day was all jangling anxiety. Though I tried to stay still. Tried not to get ahead of myself.

That evening, although it wasn't allowed and I knew it, I walked down the dirt track to Macleod Gange. *Just to take a look*, I told myself. *Just to stretch my legs.* Maybe get some socks for Naga, although I knew it was a lie. Kidding myself as I walked past the liquor stalls and then doubled back. Found myself tapping on the grille of a small wooden booth at the rear of the taxis. A kerosene lamp burnt inside. Hours later as I stumbled up the path in the dark, two men with lathis blocked the way. I couldn't put up a fight. I was no match for them. They beat me with the lathis and I gave them all I had, all the rupees in my pocket, which wasn't much. When I got back to the monastery the blood was dry on my face and it was dawn. The gong rang as I turned the key to the room and I fell into a terrifying sleep in which I wet the bed like a child and Naga appeared, a sad look on his face, and asked me to leave.

❁

I rinsed the soiled sheets, hung them out, and I was beyond shame, beyond all that. Late morning an auto arrived and I left the Retreat. I didn't look back. *This is the last time.* I didn't even have to say it, Naga knew me so well.

Back in our monastery the Abbot met me at the door, looked at my cut face and walked me to my room. Told me I must look after myself; that the doctor would come soon and I must rest. He brought water and chai and waited with me. His kindness cut me to the bone.

❁

The Tibetan doctor first checked that nothing was broken. Then he inspected my eyes and my tongue. He took hold of my wrists and tapped the veins firm with his middle finger. He tapped again and angled his head. He did not like what he heard. He spoke bluntly: 'The liver is pressing on the lung.

You've ignored this for long enough.'

'But . . .'

'You are a drinker?'

'I gave up.'

He took off his glasses and rubbed his eyes. 'When?'

'Gave up for ten years . . .'

'And now?'

'Haven't touched it for months.'

'The liver.' He started writing me a prescription. 'Your cells have gone black,' he continued, matter-of-fact. 'The symptoms show very late.' He made me promise to take the Tibetan medicine – small pills – three times a day.

'You're at the door of,' the doctor said.

'What do you mean?'

Without missing a beat he said: 'I think you know.'

I stood up and clenched my fists, shot through with adrenaline, as if I were a boy again in the village fending off attack. 'Why are you telling me all this?'

'I'm telling what I see. It's all in the pulse.'

'Who says I wanted to be told?'

He looked up at me and his voice was very calm. 'You have time to prepare. You have your training. Many do not have this.'

I sat back on the charpoy. Completely drained, I put my head in my hands. 'Tell me what to do.'

'First, you must heal your life,' he said simply. 'That door – you'll not be kept waiting forever.'

❁

The Abbot wanted me to stay but I'd made up my mind. I had to leave the monastery. Naga walked me out into the courtyard. I set down my battered suitcase and we embraced like brothers. I shut my eyes for a minute and saw all that I was leaving behind, like scenes from another life. As I turned out of the gates, it was a stark, strange world. Everything came at me bright and raw. But I felt I had to find her. Maybe find Lama; the feeling was strong. It was now or never. Fran was back in Delhi, Naga said. He'd just got a letter from her. He gave me a telephone number, said to ring it. I might find her there. 'Don't tell her anything,' I said. He nodded. He always kept his word. Time was running out. I waved once, didn't look back. Kept walking.

FRANÇOISE

Back in my old room I read the newspaper and drank chai as if I had all the time in the world; as if time had no meaning.

It would soon be the twentieth anniversary of the gas disaster. There was a story about women in Bhopal and their role in the fight for compensation. A photograph from a few years back when they'd travelled to Bombay armed with straw brooms. They'd gone to the headquarters of Dow Chemicals, the new owners of Union Carbide. 'Clean up your act,' they'd chanted. They wanted the waste cleared from the old Carbide site. 'Jahdoo Maro Dow Ko! Take a broom to Dow!' I knew that to be hit with a broom in India was a supreme insult, worse even than if someone threw a chappal. The women had gone on to the Earth Summit in South Africa with their brooms. I clipped the article to send to Naga and put it in my pocket.

I was hoping to be back in Bhopal. As soon as I could make a decision. Shahid told me that some of our work was to go on display. Funding had been extended and we were to make more work as part of a touring exhibition. I had to get back to develop the photographs.

After reading the newspapers, I couldn't delay any longer. I told Aruna I was going to Khan market. Instead I took a taxi to

Defence colony. A place Dr Chatterjee had recommended, a clinic with a bronze plaque on the door which read: B. D. Gupta. Inside there were signs everywhere high up on the walls: *Sex determination of child is not performed on these premises.*

It was clean and well-run and Mrs B. D. Gupta herself passed through the packed waiting room full of manicured women in bright silk saris. The receptionist called her over. I was directed behind a screen door. A nurse handed me a form and asked me to fill in the questions. As I went down the list and came to 'method of payment', I had a sudden flash of the tin signs hammered to trees and lamp posts around Delhi. Signs advertising abortion for five hundred rupees. This operation would cost far more than that. When the nurse came back I asked her: 'Where do those women go? The women who follow the tin signs? Where do those signs lead them?'

'Tin signs?' She looked at me strangely.

'Five hundred rupees. Out in the streets?'

She nodded. A sudden understanding. 'To a tent on the banks of the Ganga,' she informed me. 'To a basement flat in a basti. To certain infection or death. For most women in India,' she said sharply, 'five hundred rupees is a fortune.'

I nodded. 'But not here.'

'Not here. Look around you. Men outside in Range Rovers. They wait for wives or girlfriends or mistresses, for the procedure to be over.' She sighed. 'Here is for the wealthy, only.' She sighed again and looked at me hard. 'Like you.'

'I'm not wealthy,' I protested.

'Here, you are wealthy.' She was brusque and dismissive now. 'From the West.' I handed her the form and she sat down opposite me with a clipboard on her lap. She looked down at the sheet of paper preparing to tick off my answers. 'And so, tell me.' Her voice softened a little. 'For certain you do not want it?'

'No,' I said. 'I'm not at all certain.'

This startled her. She looked up. The pen hovered over the page. 'Then why are you here?'

'I want to be sure.'

'Madam. What, really, do you want?' She put down her pen. 'I'm confused.'

She started tapping her pen against the chair. 'Confused?'

'I have my life. I have my work,' I said. 'I never wanted . . .'

'Your work?'

'I'm an artist.' The words seemed grandiose. I hesitated. I was pathetic. 'I make photographs.'

'Women give birth every day,' she said in a granite voice. *Even artists.* There was contempt in her tone. 'And women every day must terminate. They have no money. No support. They cannot cope. Many reasons. What makes you so special?'

'It's not that . . .'

'But maybe,' she interrupted, 'maybe you are wasting my time here?'

I looked at her sitting there in her white coat with her calm face and beautiful teeth very white against her skin. 'Yes,' I said. 'Perhaps you're right. Of course you are.' I stood up feeling light-headed, pushed back the sliding door and out into the waiting room.

I passed a cubicle with a half-open curtain and a woman hooked up to an ultrasound, a glimpse of the monitor. Then a professional voice, apologetic: 'Most sorry, madam, a girl, most sorry. We can arrange . . .'

I said goodbye to the receptionist and blinked out into the dusty light.

✦

It was a red day of humidity and cloud. Late evening the phone rang a storm colour. I heard Aruna answer and speak rapidly in Hindi. Then she called my name. As I came down the stairs she held out the receiver. I saw that there were tears in her eyes. 'It's Sonam,' she said. 'He wants to speak with you.'

NAGA

The telephone rang through the monastery corridors. It was a cracked low voice at the end of the line, a voice I didn't recognize.

'Lakshmi?' I repeated the name.

'I'm ringing for your friend,' she said. 'The monk has news. Is saying, please hurry.'

I took the next train to Delhi and we met near the Rose Garden, across town from my old life with Memsahib and the Sardar. I noticed that most of the colonies had gates now and security cameras. All activity seemed to stop as she entered the park; the hummingbirds ceased, the cicadas fell silent. The boys paused their cricket match to stand and stare. As she walked towards me there was a collective intake of breath.

'The monk is very sick.' I heard the words come: the voice of a young man from the body of a woman.

'I know this, but I've heard nothing from him. For a month, nothing.' We sat down on a bench. My arms stayed tight across my chest. The cricket match started up again. 'Where is he?'

'He's in my tent. You must come.'

I struggled. Then I caught myself. Inside, so much judging. *A Hijra? A man-woman. Maybe a hermaphrodite, sold by her parents. Or maybe she had the cutting young? Her manhood buried under a tree? Maybe a prostitute?* My mind ran on. Above my own noise I couldn't hear clearly. 'A tent?'

'A tent.'

'Why should he be in this place?'

'This place or that place. He is wanting, only.' Her tone was impatient. 'You are helping, or . . .?'

I paused. 'Of course. I'll help you.'

'Accha.' She sat up straight, adjusted her dupatta and said, 'First he is meeting you in Chandni Chowk.'

'How can I trust you?' My tone, too sharp.

'A girl you can mistrust, but not a Hijra.' She gave me the time and the place, then fluttered a jewelled hand and walked off the way she had come.

◇

I saw him early next morning at Chandni Chowk, at the fish stalls before the day's trading began. His face had the look of someone other. He was dressed in kurta and trousers. He was thinner and frailer, although only four weeks had passed. It was clear he'd been sleeping in the streets.

'Tenzin,' I called out to him but he didn't hear. I walked up closer and moved around to his good side. I called again. He turned and put out his hand, shook his head. 'Look at me,' he said sadly. 'Tenzin is gone.'

'You are still Tenzin.'

He shrugged. 'I know you won't judge.'

'It's not for me to judge.'

'I need you to help.'

'Of course.'

We bought up all the fish we could see, all the buckets we could handle between us. The fish-wallah wasn't pleased when he saw my robes. When he saw what we were planning to do. 'No use,' said the fish-wallah. 'Later, we will catch again.'

'No bother,' Tenzin said. 'We'll pay full price.'

'But here,' the fish-wallah said, 'here, the River Yamuna is dead.'

'We will take the fish,' I insisted.

We grasped our buckets and the water patterned up our legs. Tenzin stopped many times for breath and so I helped carry his buckets also. Back and forward. In the early light the Yamuna River foamed brown at the banks. Egrets rose up from the mud and the tangle of plastic bags.

We released the fish back into the Yamuna. It was his doctor's suggestion. A gesture from one dying being to another. The splash of the bucket and the fish slid into the water and it closed around them silent as an envelope. Below the surface the fish tumbled and twined with their mouths open and gills working hard; astonished to be free.

A gesture only. The fish-wallah was right. A few hours, maybe a day, and the fish would swim out and die or be caught again, snared by a child on a low boat trailing a hook in the water. To end up again bloodied in a bucket. Or perhaps there was really another future in which the fish swam free, never again captured. The possibility of a different life.

This healing ritual of one being to another was an ancient one. 'Maybe we could buy time,' Tenzin said, 'a wee bit of time.' We stood at the water's edge and prayed. The day started up. The muezzin called the faithful and we watched the men climb the steps to the Jama Masjid and the mosque glowed red in the dawn. We walked through the market and saw the animals, everywhere in different phases of death. Animals crated, crowded, carried along with hooves tied or strung up on bamboo poles. Nearby, blood drained into a gutter from the neck of a goat.

Tenzin leant against a wall and took his medicine. 'First I must heal my life. That's what the doctor said.'

'Accha.' I held the water bottle up. 'We freed one hundred fish from slaughter.'

'Aye.' He smiled. 'But can I free myself?'

'Of course. With the right intention anything is possible.'

'Time is running out,' he said to me, 'we must find Lama Shastri. The signs are there. The dreams are there. I know where to find him. I know the person who can help us.'

He seemed to be in a fever. Maybe hallucinating. I held up my hand to stop him. 'Before all this, there is something you have forgotten.'

'What do you mean?'

'What about Françoise?' I said.

ARKAY

After I left the monastery the days passed, the weeks went by. I had her phone number in my pocket. I tried. I'd wake, dry-mouthed, on a wooden pallet not far from the Rose Garden. How did I even get here? I'd say to myself, *Today will be the day.* I will go to find her. I will make a start. My abdomen swelled and breathing was hard. I tried not to resist. I curled around the pain under my ribs. I'd come here for Fran. But it all came undone. *One more couldn't hurt.* Wait thirty seconds, sit with it, do something else. All those things I was taught. I could do it again, I told myself. I'd done it before.

The days ran on. How could I face her?

One night I had a dream of Lama Shastri. He called to me: 'I'm waiting,' he said. He clapped his hands three times. He twirled in the air. The dream was vivid. I knew I was dreaming. There was a sunset light – a red candle on a low table. Cow dung burnt from a brazier. I rushed towards the light. There was a woman in that light and a man also. The woman and man were on a bed. I watched them. I wanted to join them. I watched as the man pulled out, parted her, his tongue played with her, he put one, two, three fingers inside. She spread her thighs wide. I saw the pink flushing to red. He slowly withdrew his fingers and then re-entered at the end of her coming. He closed his eyes as he started to come; her legs were over his shoulders. It was Fran, I knew that much.

Then Lama appeared again. He spoke of a child. His form kept changing. There was the sound of bells. Now he was a beautiful pillar of light and limbs flowed from the pillar. Now a woman, now a man. I followed the sunset light over a city of mosques and lakes. I heard a dholak drum sound my name. I heard a hollow-palmed clapping.

Then I woke up.

I shook myself, moved my toes, checked down my body. Limbs still intact. My hand connected with the last bottle of Cobra, knocked it over, and the amber spilled out. My head ached as I put my tongue down to the dirt and so I reached out a finger. I lifted my index finger to my tongue.

It was dawn and a red-eyed dog circled near. For no reason, I started to weep. There were the tablets in my pocket – my medicine – and I looked around for some water. Other men roused from sleep outside the park.

How did I get here?

Days and nights like this since I left the monastery. Since she left me. Or I left her; I couldn't make sense of it any more. And nothing, no amount of drink seemed to help. It wouldn't let up; my breath came in short and I was unsteady on my feet. *One more couldn't hurt.*

So many days and nights. But the dream was a sign, after so many nights without dreams. It couldn't go on. I sat up, the taste of mud and alcohol in my mouth.

I walked slowly round the park trying to work it all out. By then it was late morning and rain started to fall. Just outside the fence, across the road, I saw a woman on the ground and a taxi-wallah standing over her, fists raised. 'Bas,' she cried, in a low voice. 'Bas.' I could've kept walking but I crossed the road, ignored the taxi-wallahs and the blare of horns. Almost ran into a young boy, horizontal with the weight of a container on his back. An older man followed, a Sikh. He called out to the domestic, 'Jigme!' in a loud voice. He walked with sticks. He edged around the woman at his feet. 'Jigme!' He called again and then, 'Taxi!' As the taxi door shut he saw me and for a second we looked at each other. He leant forward as if he knew me. I turned away and lifted the woman to her feet – close up, I saw that she was a Hijra – brushed the mud from her shalwaar kameez, ignored the catcalls of the men.

'My name is Lakshmi,' she said.

The Hijra's forehead was cut, her nose bled. A rickshaw drove past and slowed down. She clutched some rupee notes in her palm and showed them to the driver. The rickshaw-wallah paused for a moment, inclined his head and pedalled off. She looked up at me and I took the money and hailed an auto, took her to the Tibetan doctor in Nizamuddin. I left her at a tent along the main road leading away from the gardens. She used to live in the bath house along with the other Hijras but had argued with the main chela, she said. She had been living in this tent for months.

'Stay,' she said. 'I must thank you.' She lit a brazier and heated a saucepan of water for chai. Then she sat on a stool with her mirror and her tweezers, absorbed in her reflection, and started talking. She told me she wasn't a man; she wasn't a woman either. She was born this way. She never had the cutting to become a Hijra. She was a dancer, she said. At weddings. At the birth of children. Named for the goddess Lakshmi who brings wealth and good fortune. She spoke of her guru Bahuchara Mata, the guru of all Hijras. Her families were Dalits, she said. They had converted to Buddhism to escape their caste. The Hijras had come for her at thirteen and her family had signed the papers. She always prayed to both Buddha and to Bahuchara Mata for a better life she said.

She had these dreams and Bollywood ideas. Sometimes she went with men for money, she said, only sometimes. Then she raised an eyebrow and gave me a look and I held up my hand, 'Oh no. That's not why I'm here.'

I told her why I was in Delhi: how I'd come to find my guru, his incarnation, but I'd gone off track. I'd come also to find a woman, Françoise. I just needed to rest and to sort myself out then make a start.

I told her I was a monk. I said she could call me Arkay.

She said I could rest in her tent and I fell into a deep sleep and woke the next day. When I opened my eyes, Lakshmi was standing there over the charpoy with a garland in her hands and a look on her face.

'I'm not cut out to be a bridegroom,' I said.

She stood in the doorway with the marigold garland looped through her fingers, a dholak drum in one hand. She clapped three times, a special hollow-palm clap, and said: 'Don't enjoy sadly.'

I sat up. In the half-light I knew why I'd been led to this place.

NAGA

I rang the bell. I heard it ringing up the steps past the large wooden Ganesha at the entrance, ringing up to the first floor with the dusted portraits and unopened books; ringing up into the kitchen. I checked my watch. It was 3 p.m. Again I rang the bell. I walked up the marble steps, lifting my robes with my right hand. I stood outside the wrought-iron screen. I waited, for some minutes I waited. Then I remembered. Old Memsahib always had chai at this time. Another minute and a small boy, no more than fifteen, opened the wooden door behind the screen. He squinted. Mosquitoes buzzed around my head as I stood in the entrance and the daylight flared down behind me. I leant forward. 'Miss Françoise?'

'Ek moment,' he said backing away from the screen, locking it again. Memsahib came to the door, much older now, still handsome, with a grey streak in her hair just like Indira. She peered through the wire screen at my robes, at my shaven head, and opened the door a fraction.

'Memsahib,' I said, a little nervous after all this time. And then, in English: 'How are you?' Something in my voice. She moved closer and searched my face, saw the purple marks more clearly.

'Sonam!' She used my old name. 'Sonam,' she repeated. She

grasped my hand with her two hands, pulled me into the room. Her eyes were full. 'Please – come in, come in. Françoise is expecting you. This is wonderful!' She pulled me into the room of familiar coolness, scuffed marble floors and antiques in cabinets. My eye accustomed itself and everything was as I remembered. I looked with the eye of a domestic, the practised eye which anticipates every need. There was a large crack in the plaster of the ceiling, much larger than before. A spider-web trailed loose in one corner. The rugs on the floor were faded and frayed along one edge. My eye roamed the house as if at any moment I would be asked to pick up a dustcloth or a brush.

Memsahib, meanwhile, was studying me. I could see that she was impressed with my robes, impressed that I was heavier, a grown man now. And something from the past rose inside me, memories of being a *boy* in this house. I noted the feeling, rising and passing, the heat across my chest. I told myself that Memsahib always tried to be kind. She always did her best, what she was able to do. She motioned to follow her upstairs, to the drawing room. She called for drinks. 'Chai?' she asked me. 'Nimbu pani? You will have?'

I delighted in the feel of the seat with its tapestry material. On rare afternoons when the house was empty I used to sit on these chairs, watch myself sitting there in the brass mirror opposite and run my fingers along, finding loose threads, tracing the patterns. Now here I was, a guest in this house. Pride rose in me, a hot, unaccustomed feeling that I held fast to, I'd worked hard for, I did not want to let go.

'Nimbu pani,' I said, grateful because I was very thirsty. I watched as the domestic came in minutes later, his brown bare feet soundless on the marble floor, wrestling with a wooden tray bigger than his arms.

'Sonam! But this is not your name any more?' Memsahib flushed.

'Nagarjuna,' I said. 'My name is Naga.'

'Naga,' she repeated. 'What to say?' Tears again came to her eyes. 'I'm sorry . . .' She trailed off. 'Forgive me. Your family. I'm so sorry, you must believe. We didn't want to lose you.' She sighed. 'But you've found your own path.' She lifted her cup of chai in my honour and passed samosa, brinjal, roast pumpkin seeds, which I declined.

'Memsahib.' I leant forward. I continued in English. 'Please. There is nothing to forgive. The past is past.' I paused. 'The money in the envelope. I must thank you. It paid for my sister's funeral.'

Memsahib nodded and wiped her eyes. 'I'm so sorry,' she repeated. Then she straightened up, gestured around the room and said brightly, 'As you can see, here, nothing changes.' She shook her head sadly. 'Although Sahib's pain is much worse now, much worse, in his legs and feet and in his lungs. And Old Memsahib!' Here she lowered her voice. 'She will outlive us all!'

The domestic handed me my nimbu pani. I tasted the lime, the sugar. I held it, the tartness and sweetness on my tongue. Suddenly I realized that I was enjoying myself.

'Who would have thought?' said Memsahib looking again at my robes, my shaven head.

'Jigme,' she addressed the servant boy. 'Tell Miss Françoise she has a visitor.'

I shifted a little in my seat and adjusted my robes. I left this house with nothing. All was different now and I felt myself wanting to feel esteemed. I saw this balloon up. This wanting to make Memsahib feel small. I struggled to push it away. I closed my eyes to calm myself.

Moments later I heard the elephant bells on the back of the guest door, footsteps on the stairs. Françoise looked over the balustrade. She paused, ran down the last few steps and grasped my hands in hers as if it were only the day before and not so much in between.

'Naga,' she said, and her eyes were shining.

'You're here.' I stood up bowing, awkward. We both laughed to hide our confusion and sadness.

We sat for a while drinking chai and talking, then Françoise suggested we go outside, get some air, walk around the small park at the edge of the colony.

I said goodbye to Memsahib. 'You are always welcome,' she said. 'Please, do not forget us. Please – come back soon.' She said this with great sincerity and I nodded. For a moment we both believed it could happen.

I walked outside with Françoise. The light was fading, the streetlights were coming on and people were walking in the cool of early evening, wrapping their shawls about.

'It's Tenzin,' I said to her. 'He's very ill. He's dying. He wants very much to see you.'

She stopped in the middle of the narrow path. She put her hand to her belly. Her voice was calm, there was no surprise. She looked down at the cracked paving stone at her feet, at the three-legged dog near the magnolia bushes. 'He's been dying for a long time.'

'Yes,' I said. 'Please come.'

She looked away from me then and put her hands up to her face.

❀

'It happens,' I told her. 'How easily it happens. All the training, all those years, can fall, like that.' I spoke from the heart. I spoke from my own experience. How lost I had felt after my sister. 'Back in the monastery he was unsettled, unhappy, all of us could see. What to say?' I looked at her. 'It was the old problem.'

'And then?'

'I gave him your number. He came to Delhi. But the illness took hold. Then Lakshmi . . .'

'Lakshmi?' Françoise frowned and tried to absorb all that I was telling her.

'The Hijra.' I shrugged. 'Tenzin believes she will lead us to Lama's incarnation.'

Françoise looked away across the park at the beginnings of a cricket match taking shape, all the boys in the street assembling. 'Do you believe that?'

'What is important is that he believes.'

'Naga, what should I do?'

'You should see him. You can tell him . . .'

'I'm confused.'

'Then tell him that.'

'I was going to send a letter . . .'

'Too late for this. He left weeks ago. He left to find you,' I repeated.

Françoise hesitated. 'He came to Delhi? To find me?'

'Yes.'

'But he didn't even look.'

'Please,' I said. 'Françoise.'

'Why should I see him?'

'It's your decision. But if you come, I'll be there.' I gave her a map, hand-drawn. 'Regards once more to Memsahib,' I said. 'To Sahib also.'

She smiled at the mention of Sahib. 'He'll be sorry he missed you.'

She took a folded newspaper article from her pocket. 'This is for you,' she said. 'For your files.' She watched me hail an auto, watched the wheels spin in the yellow dusk light and waved until she could no longer see me, then turned slowly back to the house and up the marble steps.

FRANÇOISE

At breakfast next morning Surjit couldn't resist, couldn't help himself. As he passed the fruit bowl, he said, 'I always knew you'd come back for a Sherpa or a monk.'

'Surjit!' Aruna waved a hand at him.

'You were right all along,' I said. Too weary to argue.

'I must tell you something else,' he said. 'This monk of yours, I think we know him.'

I took a sip of my chai. 'Oh?' I looked down at the plate of food but had no appetite.

'I'm sure it must be the same fellow. Saw him again, weeks back. It was raining and I tried to hail an auto, sent Jigme ahead with the water container and this chap ran across the road – could have got himself killed – almost knocked Jigme over, then he stooped down, this fellow, because there was someone on the ground and a taxi-wallah making a tamasha. A woman on the ground, at least I thought . . .'

'But it wasn't a woman,' Aruna interrupted.

'Thank you, Aruna.' He lowered his chin and furrowed at her over his reading glasses. 'Thank you! How my wife loves to finish my sentences. It wasn't a woman at all, but a damn Hijra. Imagine! They're all prostitutes, not to be trusted . . .'

'Where was this?' I cut him off.

'Near the Rose Garden.' Surjit paused. 'Yes, that's where it was.'

'Maybe it wasn't him.' I shook my head and reached for some water. I wasn't sure of anything.

'Well,' Surjit continued. 'Reminded me of a chap, a guest here, years ago. I never forget a face. Anyway, tall, this fellow. Thin. Shaved head. In fact, I think I saw him not in robes at all one day. I saw him' – he looked around the table – 'drinking. At a stall near Chandni Chowk.'

'Surjit!' Aruna implored him to stop.

He looked at me closely to see if he'd hit the target.

Aruna turned to me, rolled her eyes. 'It could've been anyone, Surjit. There's more than one firangi monk in Delhi.'

'More than one firangi drunk?' Surjit was triumphant, enjoying his own wit.

'What did he look like?' Despite myself, I had to ask.

'Very fair. More than this, I can't remember.' Surjit paused for effect, splayed his palms on the table. He lowered his chin and opened his eyes wide: 'They all look the same, these foreigners.'

I left the house late afternoon. Surjit stood in the doorway. He wanted to lecture me I was certain of it, but I didn't give him a chance. I tried to slip past but Aruna stopped me.

'Wait,' she said. 'I've told him everything.'

'Everything?'

She nodded. 'Yes.'

'You must bring him here,' said Surjit. He put an arm round my shoulders: 'In this house, you are like a daughter. The friend of our daughter must not die on the street.'

'You must bring him,' Aruna repeated. 'The Old Memsahib is away. She's with her daughter in Haryana. You can bring him here.'

I nodded and said goodbye and kept my head low as I walked past them and down the steps. I felt a little unsteady, my centre of gravity shifting. Aruna arranged a driver and the car was already there; a bunch of plastic grapes swung silver from the mirror. I showed Naga's hand-drawn map to the driver. As we turned out of the colony and into the streets, I tried to focus on the life passing outside. I saw a row of signs, red-and-white metal attached to trees like memorial plaques:

ABORTION UP TO EIGHT WEEKS

Each sign had a telephone number and a price underneath. For a moment, I hesitated. As we stopped at another intersection, and yet another tin sign, I took out a pen and wrote down the number. Although I knew it was too late, already weeks too late. I crumpled the paper in my pocket. Then another huge road sign called out:

KILLER DRIVING. DELHI LEADS THE WAY IN ROAD DEATH

The driver thought it was funny and laughed and pointed. I smiled with him as he threaded through the traffic, displaying his skill. The streetlamps came on. I saw women wheeling barrows of stone along the road by kerosene lamp, bricks piled high on their heads. Construction workers with torn sari blouses. All along the road people were living in tents with washing lines strung from trees. Through a mud brick wall with a small gate I glimpsed a man lying on a charpoy watching colour television. Men forged hammers around a metal-bin furnace. Women sold limes from wicker baskets; they sold marigold garlands looped from tree branches. A man washed, soaping himself under his loincloth and rinsing himself from an old plastic bucket. Children tumbled in the dirt. A woman at a roundabout peeled fruit for the baby at her breast.

Orange gas cylinders chimed loudly, balanced on the back of old bicycles. As we slowed down at the next intersection there was an old man selling raffia mats. Tyres and wheels hung low in the trees. The green and gold rickshaws tambourined through me, shaking through the traffic.

Before a fork in the road I saw a row of tents. I looked again at Naga's map. This must be it. 'Bas. Rukhiye,' I said, in my minimal Hindi, alerting the driver to stop. I stumbled over uneven ground past kerosene lamps and rows of dried cow dung to the first tent. A thin man squatted outside and shook his head at me, languidly flicked his wrist to direct me further along. I stepped up to a green tarpaulin and called Arkay's name. A familiar voice answered, urging me inside. It was Naga and he stood up as I entered, clasped my hand and sat down again. He motioned for me to sit on a wooden crate. A woman in a purple-and-gold sari had her back to me and did not turn around.

Under the tarpaulin it was dark. A butter lamp sputtered down. A small brazier illuminated one corner. Instinctively I drew my camera up.

THE TENT

A thin man lies on a charpoy, his face turned to the wall. A brazier burns in one corner. A prayer wheel rests on a small crate next to him.

New Delhi, January 2005

NAGA

'You could be in the monastery,' I said to him. 'You could be in a hospital.'

'Aye,' he said.

'But you chose here?'

'This chose me.'

'You are sure?'

'I'm sure. And I stopped the drink.'

'Yes.'

He tried to laugh, lay weak on the charpoy. 'Stopped in plenty time to die.'

'We must prepare,' I said. I lit the brazier. I took Lakshmi's broom from the corner and swept the dirt floor.

Tenzin leant back on the cushions watching me move around the tent.

'Naga?'

'Yes.'

'The doctor spoke of a door. What do you think? What is really behind it?'

I stopped sweeping and put the broom down. 'Everything.'

'All the people I hurt? All the people I ever made happy?'

'There is nothing to fear. If you can stay steady.'

'I've had glimpses.'

'Yes?'

'In meditation. In drink. In friendship and love. Times when everything flowed. When there was no separation. No *this* or *that*.'

'Then you know what is behind the door.'

'But can I face it?'

I squatted next to the charpoy. 'Sit with whatever the mind throws.'

'I don't know if I can.'

I smiled at him. 'You've done it before.'

'Naga. Please. When the time comes. Help me not to run.'

I put my hand on his shoulder. 'I will help you.'

He smiled, hesitated then he closed his eyes and his hand fell back on the charpoy.

'Anyway,' he said. 'Why should my death be any different?'

'You're from the West. You have choices. You could be in the hospital.' I crushed the painkillers and mixed them with water as the Hijra had instructed. I pounded the tablets. I was full of anger. 'Why this Lakshmi?' I said, my tone too harsh. 'I don't understand.'

'She can lead us to Lama,' he said. 'All the signs are there. The signs from his cremation. From my dreams . . .'

'This could mean anything.'

'Naga. I believe she can lead us to Lama. There is a family . . .'

'If you believe,' I said, picking up the broom again and sweeping the dust through the gap in the tarpaulin. I could see my friend on the far bank. Already he was gone. I kept sweeping. The winter light hard and cold in my eyes.

FRANÇOISE

It took some minutes to adjust in the low light. Lakshmi leant over the charpoy. Naga introduced us and she looked over at me and pressed her lips together. Her over-painted mouth was angled down.

Arkay half-opened his eyes when he heard my voice. He smiled. 'It's you,' he said, and for a moment we were both happy.

'I got caught up,' he said. 'Messed up. But believe me. I wanted to find you.' His voice was strained and pale; he turned his face to the wall. Lakshmi cleared her throat.

'Yes,' I said, biting my lip. 'I know all that.'

Suddenly he said: 'What colour do you hear?'

I paused. Shut my eyes. 'Is this a test?'

Then quite unexpectedly he said: 'I'm sorry.'

Lakshmi grew so big; with every movement she seemed to fill the space. Then my hand was on her arm, pleading with her: 'Please, let me do something. Let me help.'

She crushed painkillers, mixed them in water and pressed them to his mouth with a face cloth. She turned round slowly.

'You want to help?' She put the cloth in the water, wrung it out and placed it on Arkay's hot forehead.

'Please,' I said. 'He should be in a hospital. He should be somewhere else.'

'You're not in West now.'

Naga watched us closely. 'Sit, only. Be still. This is best. For the dying mind, this is best.'

Lakshmi set the face cloth down on the edge of the bucket. She squatted, staking her position next to the pillow. The only place for me was at the end of the charpoy. I reached out and touched Arkay's bruised left foot protruding from the sheet. I rested my hand there. His leg was cool as marble. Naga smiled at me, an amused smile.

'Sit,' he said. 'Be still.'

Arkay rubbed his eyes. 'My colour's a little better today.'

His colour was bad. His skin was yellow. He was yellow as a drumbeat to me. I saw the edge of a mirror shining on the dirt floor and a pair of tweezers next to it. I looked over at Lakshmi. The mirror and the tweezers must be hers. She must show him his reflection. I hesitated. 'Yes,' I soothed. 'I'm sure your colour is a little better.'

I look over at Naga. He nodded encouragement, then he said quietly, 'I must get water.' Lakshmi followed him out with an armful of plastic bottles.

I closed my eyes. Resentment rose up into lime-bitter focus: 'You treated me badly,' I said to Arkay. 'You hurt me. You hurt me a lot.'

'Maybe you wanted to be hurt?'

I rested my forehead on the edge of the charpoy. 'No one wants to be hurt.'

'Sometimes we go looking for pain.'

It was my opportunity. I wanted to tell him about the child.

'Believe me, Fran, I'm sorry.'

Naga returned to the tent carrying the refilled bottles. Lakshmi came in with another butter lamp.

'I heard voices,' Naga said to me.

'We were speaking.'

Naga frowned. 'You can speak,' he said. 'But don't disturb him. Let him rest. He has a long long journey to come.'

Then I told them about Surjit's offer. Lakshmi gestured around; her long fingers twisted the damp cloth. Then she threw the cloth in the bucket and strode out of the tent. For a moment I hesitated, looked over at Naga. I knew what I had to do. I was determined. I pushed back the tarpaulin and followed her out.

NAGA

This time I do not notice the rugs or the cobwebs in the corner. I do not see my old self in the scuff of the marble floor because this is the end now and I must focus. My friend in the centre of this room, everything settles on this moment.

I try to remember all I've ever learnt. With the dying, time has a different meaning. The moments reach from breath to breath, like tightropes. We balance on these breaths. Past and future dissolve. We see time for what it truly is. Again and again Tenzin kicks off the sheet like a sick child, limbs in slow motion. He reaches out first one hand and then the other. He opens his eyes. 'The green light.' He points to a corner of the room and a glass-fronted cabinet.

'A green light?' I repeat, trying to soothe.

He kicks off the sheet with one foot and we try to ease it back. He kicks it off again. His upper torso and head are warm to the touch, fevered almost, but his legs are black and cold.

'Over there,' he says, falling back on the pillow but keeping his arm extended.

He brings his hand back to his face and closes his eyes. He scratches his skin, back and forth across the stubble on his face. 'Insects,' he says, 'everywhere.'

He struggles to hoist himself up and Françoise steps forward. We take hold of him under the shoulders, lift, we adjust the

pillows then he lies back, heaving with the effort. Françoise tries
to press water to his mouth but he can no longer swallow.

In the last hours his face thins. Everything in his face stretches
back as if death is pressing him down onto the charpoy and from
there into the earth. On the right side of his face a bruise forms
at the hairline. I notice all the changes. The Sahib and
Memsahib come and go. They instruct Jigme to bring chai.
Sahib limps in with an armful of towels and sponges. Memsahib
brings in bowls of fruit, opens the window a little more. She
brings candles and places them around the charpoy.

Tenzin's bowels run and Memsahib lights more incense and
a frangipani scent rises up. We try to lift him, wash him down.

We sit like this, waiting. Reciting from the Book of the Dead
and observing the signs.

Small changes, minute by minute. His breath slows. There's
a hard sound at the back of his throat then his breath comes dry
and he opens his eyes a little and it's another change, as if a large
animal has entered the room after great effort and flung itself at
our feet, panting in the heat of an afternoon.

I pass my hand over his damp hair, there's still some heat at
the crown, but the rest of his body is cold. I keep one hand on
his right arm and it chills me through the sheet.

We keep vigil at the end of the charpoy. I turn a prayer wheel
and chant; try to speed his consciousness to a pure place.

'Soon,' I say, out loud. 'Soon it is coming.'

❀

I look at the grandfather clock. It's past midnight. I slow my
breath right down and look through the window into the dark.

There's a space outside lit by a streetlamp. In that space I see figures moving. Westerners. I see their silhouettes against the wall. There's a milkcart and young boys loading empty crates. They are talking and laughing but there's no sound. Then the scene changes: a young woman in a car, sun through a windscreen. She checks the rear mirror waiting for a man who never returns. I rub my eyes. There's a young boy drinking from one bottle, then another. He crawls across the snow. Another man carves into a block of onyx, throws out his hands to bless the day.

Tenzin is restless. I have merged with his mindstream. I try to stay steady.

Dark shapes appear, animal and human, they crowd the window blocking the street light. I take a deep breath. *This is fear*, I say to myself. The dark shapes crowd over and around the charpoy. His mind is agitated. I grip his shoulder, urge him to stay strong. *This is only fear.* My mind and his mind. *Do not run.* Suddenly the dark shapes shimmer and spark, fade altogether. Then Lama appears and the words drum through:

I was born in a Scottish mining village halfway between Glasgow and Edinburgh.

I was born on the Nepali border. My mother ate munacka for the pain.

I was born in a hospital with wet curtains. Two lilies burst open in a vase.

I was born neither man nor woman. I did not need the cutting.

I have been born in so many places.

I put my hands up to shield me from the light.

'Are you OK?' Françoise asks.

When I look down at the charpoy Tenzin is lying on his left side facing us. He opens his eyes. His gaze arcs over the room.

His eyes kaleidoscope – all colours, beautiful – his gaze fixes and he smiles with effort and we smile back and for that moment we are all one face, one smile. Then his eyes shut and blood trails from the left side of his mouth.

I move to the top of the charpoy and place my hand on the crown of his head. I take a small cup filled with dark liquid and touch a spoonful to his mouth. I give him the last food of the Buddhist rites. I read from the Book of the Dead.

I close the book and concentrate on the small prayer wheel. I raise it and rotate it above the charpoy. 'OM MANI PADME HUNG,' I say, feeling the warmth of the candles and the flame of the mantra inside.

FRANÇOISE

I caught her wrist. 'Lakshmi, wait.'

She spun around. 'You are wanting to take him away?'

'We think it's best.'

'For you? The monk is here for a reason.'

'He's dying.'

'He is here to find his teacher.' She paused.

'Lakshmi. We don't have time. We need to make him comfortable.'

She turned away. 'You don't understand.'

'That's right. I don't understand.'

'I am here to help, only. You do not trust . . .'

'Lakshmi, please.' I gave her directions to the house. 'Please,' I repeated.

'Take him,' she said, her voice indigo with resignation. 'This place or that place? I am caring for him. Now is the letting go. This is what the Buddha teaches. I am the messenger, only. The monk knows this. I know this. One day you will understand.'

❁

Just after midnight we brought Arkay from the tent. The driver helped carry him up the marble steps through the heavy door. The incense was freshly lit and the charpoy was ready and we lowered Arkay on to it with the family portraits staring down, generations of them, and the dark heavy furniture solid in the room.

Naga and I exchanged glances. Surjit leant on his stick with his back to the wall. He brought his hands up in namaste when we entered. He didn't say anything. It seemed as if nothing would ever surprise him, that this was how it had to be in this moment. He had lived through things I could never imagine. He dealt with things as they came. He believed in helping those close to him. He believed in kindness to strangers. Aruna covered the mirrors and lit small candles all the way along the stairs. Jigme came and went through the swing door from the kitchen with water and chai and fresh towels.

I listened to the dull sound of the grandfather clock and watched Arkay with a concentration I never knew I had, alert to every change of breath or movement. Naga kept vigil at the end of the charpoy and we took turns, reading from the Book of the Dead.

◊

In a shutter-click of time how a life changes.

I took out my camera. It seemed the most natural thing.

Light edged the window. It was dawn and the sky was all discs and swirls, the clouds long and dark and smudged at the seams. The sun strained through and I framed it like that: light over the charpoy and a shadow lying there. I walked out onto the balcony. Near the lamp post I saw a tall figure in a pink sari, a large flower in her hair. She had a drum at her feet. When she saw me she raised her hands up. She twirled slowly and clapped three times.

THE CHILD

A monk carries a small urn. He stands in front of a stone doorway carved with scenes from the life of the Buddha.

Sanchi, Madhya Pradesh, February 2005

NAGA

I got off the bus first; the small urn knocked against my hip. I waited for Françoise and helped her down the steps then we walked together up towards the stupas. A group of young boys played cricket behind the low wire fence. Circles of cow dung dried in rows.

We went through the wire gate past the guard in khaki with the red-badged cap. I sat on the stone steps of the old boundary wall and looked out over green fields and the slope of the hills and quietly chanted OM three times. The sound vibrated through me filling every space. In the distance there was the blast of the train horn; the racket of wheels along steel.

Françoise walked on ahead. I got up slowly. This day, my feet were giving me trouble. I walked towards the first stupa, the great stupa with its four toranas – stone gates carved with scenes from the life of the Buddha. I stopped before an empty marble throne. It was from the time before the Buddha took form. The time before representation. I walked through the monastery ruins. A gecko slid down a headless figure. I saw piles of marble and granite, everything incomplete, and as I was about to turn away I came upon a carved foot embedded in a small block of stone. I leant down to touch the stone, the square toes of the

Buddha, a fragment out of time. I knelt down and placed my forehead there and rested for some minutes. For many lives, I rested.

I looked around for Françoise. I wanted to show her these things.

It was my return visit. All these years in between. We walked slowly in the sunlight around the three stupas. I opened my arms to bless the day. I took the urn out of my bag, opened it a little, and the ashes lifted on a light breeze.

I felt the past fall away. All of it. There was only the presence and the absence of our friend. His struggle. There was only this moment. Beyond anger or sorrow or sadness.

I handed the urn to Françoise. She walked towards the main torana. When she was finished she put the empty urn on the ground and spread her arms wide. She gave me her camera and asked me to take a photograph.

It was over two months since the December anniversary, the twentieth anniversary of Bhopal. Every time I'd opened a newspaper the face of the Chairman stared back. Once again there had been calls for extradition, but he was an old man now. Maybe too late. Maybe too frail.

I sorted through my files and folded the newspapers away. I was weary. Moving to the cushion, I sat in my accustomed place by the window. I sat with my eyes half-closed and felt the breath flow up my left side, down the right. I focused on the point between my eyes and looked out through this third-eye place. For the first time I softened. I reached out to Anderson. In the wake of this December anniversary I truly felt his difficulties, knew his all-too-human pain, knew how it was and what would one day happen. I breathed into a final image of him. The end that he could never escape.

May he be at peace, I said to myself. *May he be ready.*

◇

I see a garden in America. An old man pruning roses. He puts the shears down, takes a postcard from his pocket, looks at it for the second time that morning and shakes his head. On one side, the old image: the unknown child and his own face next to it, black-framed. For twenty years that connection. He curses loudly as he turns the card over. *What the?* On the other side a message, handwritten:

HANG ANDERSON

He rubs his forehead, confused. *After all this time?* he asks himself. As he gets to his feet he drops the card, grinds it under his heel, cuts some roses for his wife. She adores pink roses.

Then Anderson looks around, sees it coming. 'I'm an old man,' he pleads.

The pain arrows from his skull and down his left arm. He falls to the ground with the gardening shears in his right hand. The pain rams hard around his heart. He falls, the flowers against his chest. When he wakes he sees the roses crushed and the thorns in his palm but no blood. His mind runs. He wakes into the past, into a grey cloud, the sound of a thousand feet.

A siren warns into him, high-pitched, although he knows the switch is turned off. He's dragged through rusting machinery and corroded safety valves. He's dragged past tank #610, slowly leaking. He starts to choke. He's in a force field pushing him down. He enters a three-tiered grave and sees the child up-close: the child with opaque eyes staring up from the dirt, the child in the famous photograph; the child who has stalked his dreams for years.

He moves through an old man with his family bent double, praying, out past the railway tracks. Their mouths and heads are covered. He steps through bodies blistered and split. Then a hospital ward full of bodies. He picks up a blue foetus with wrinkled skin. It slides from his hand and into a large jar. Next to it, in another jar, another foetus stares out from a milky eye in the middle of its forehead. A doctor swings past. 'Children of the gas kaand,' he says, pointing to the jars.

Then Anderson is pulled forward through time – twenty years – back to the present. He's in the city of mosques and lakes. He joins the daily trek of thousands across the city and waits in line to get medicine. He finds himself in a queue for money at the government office. He waits eight hours without water and food to be told that he does not have the correct papers. A government doctor must verify the diseases he claims for. He returns again the next month and the next, for a decade he returns, a decade spasms in an instant, always to be told the same thing. He is chained to a group of women with ruined eyesight and ruined wombs selling off bridal jewellery in exchange for medicine.

He sees an old man tending a grave: 'Here lies my son,' says the old man, pointing to his heart. 'I spent life savings on his treatment.'

This force drags him down. Anderson closes his eyes. He asks himself: *Where am I? What place is this?* Then the answer comes as the earth opens up to greet him, the name of the city forms in blood-red letters, spreads like gas over a lake.

It comes for him, in the shape of a familiar man in a dark suit. Mouthing the name of that city, two syllables, a briefcase and a mound of pesticide in his hand. 'In exchange for this,' he says, pointing to Anderson's body, 'I will give you that.' His arms spread wide revealing the life to come. The pesticide runs like salt through his fingers. The powder sizzles on the ground. Anderson drinks from a poisoned well, his tongue and throat turn fire, a rash flares across his skin. His eyes grow blind. Anderson becomes a permanent refugee, away from the city of mosques and lakes, away from his summerhouse in Florida. He's no longer a corporate fugitive pruning his rose garden, waiting to be caught.

I watch as he starts to run into this future stretching before him. A future in which he has no pause for breath. A future in which he can never stop running. To never escape this wheel of samsara. My heart opens to Anderson.

'May he be ready,' I say out loud. 'May he one day find peace.'

I get up from meditation. Move around the room. I sift through the papers and files and boxes of newspaper clippings piled in the corner and I lift them, one by one, years of my life so heavy with it, and I walk out to a path near the stream to an old metal container for burning and throw everything in. At that moment the Abbot walks by. He sees what I am doing and we smile at each other, bow in namaste. We stand watching, silent, until the paper catches and the wind blows the smoke into the distance.

A small child dances in the centre of a cramped room. There is a large statue of the Buddha and a row of bowls and cymbals on the dirt floor.

New Delhi, February 2005

FRANÇOISE

From Sanchi I returned to Delhi. I packed the empty urn away. The passage of time rang white and slow. I took no photographs but I took note of my distractions: when I wanted to run, when I wanted to sit. Mostly, I wanted to run. There were many days when I'd see myself falling. I'd see the blood sound, hoped this would happen. I'd lift heavy objects and pray for a reprieve, for some accident of nature. This went on for weeks. Nothing I did made any difference.

Aruna watched me closely. 'You must accept,' she said, 'all that has happened. It's too late. You can only go forward.'

'Can I?'

'You have no choice.'

I seemed to forget everything I'd ever learnt in meditation. How to sit, how not to struggle. But every morning I walked, and this became my meditation. I'd get up early and splash my face with water. Get my hat and sunglasses and try to open the door quietly, but as I turned the handle the string of Rajasthani bells always rang gold. I'd walk downstairs in my bare feet carrying my shoes. Most mornings I'd see Jigme coming down the barsati steps with washing piled in his arms.

It was the familiar symphony, this walking. The practised movements, everyone joining in at precise moments and all the colours of the day contained in that park. The old paan seller would wave to me from outside the gates and I'd wave back. The early morning cricket match was in full swing and I was conspicuous yet again as the only foreigner here. A firangi woman, obviously pregnant and alone. Yet I felt comfortable. The colony had absorbed me. A neighbour walked slowly around the park with his small girl child on his shoulders remarking on the hibiscus in bloom, directing her attention to the plants and flowers. They smiled and waved. They looked very happy. Perhaps it could be that easy, I thought. That kind of happiness.

What could be simpler or more elemental, I tried to convince myself, than a parent and a child?

❁

A sweeper with a splayed straw broom shifted dust from one side of the street to the other. I saw Jigme walk out of the front gate and approach her. He counted with his fingers, negotiating the fee. The street sweeper nodded, looked left and right, alert for council inspectors, and followed Jigme upstairs. The street remained half-swept.

From the park I'd retrace my journey around the block. Schoolgirls now made their way in clusters towards the school gates. They wore white shalwaar kameez with blue dupattas; blue ribbons at the end of dark braids. They clutched folders and books to their chests, chattering like a flock of beautiful colourful birds.

Children, that's what I noticed. Children everywhere.

❁

Outside the Parliament building a man sang of the Nehru dynasty. 'Nehru, father,' he called, 'all praise to you. Indira, Sanjay, Rajiv. None can match you.' He sang in Hindi and English. The singer was a tall man with long white hair swept off his forehead. He wore thick black-rimmed glasses and dressed in layers of blue and grey. He carried a large stick and tapped it on the ground with each alternate step. I took a shot of his feet and his long shadow. I sat at a chai stall close to the Parliament building, near rows of cars and a man getting his hair cut. The man balanced on an uneven chair in front of a mirror nailed to a tree. Clumps of dark hair slid to the ground. As the man tilted his face to check his reflection, the chair tilted with him.

Everything was seamless as I sat there with the song's lilt. There was the blue sound of the stick hitting the dirt; the colours of car exhaust; the scissors slicing through my sadness and the bright sensation in my belly. Despite myself, the world was coming back to me.

I hailed a taxi to Old Delhi. I wanted to see the new Metro. Near its hoardings, I shot a row of red-and-white fire buckets suspended on hooks from a metal rod, arranged like an art installation. Monkeys played around the buckets and peeled bananas. They ran along the concrete walls, abandoning the peels to the street below. A small child sat at the foot of the wall collecting the scraps.

How did the child survive? I asked myself. *Where did she live? Where was her family?*

I found myself, quite unexpectedly, weeping for her mother. Weeping for all mothers.

✿

I went with Naga to see Lakshmi. I met him at New Delhi station and from there we caught a taxi to Chandni Chowk. It was
early morning. Mist clung heavy to the ground. Children passed
in cycle rickshaws – public-school rickshaws – the children in
red blazers and blue uniforms, bright against the haze. Once
again I was surrounded by children. The rickshaw-wallahs
rubbed their hands to keep warm. Elegant women with brief-
cases adjusted their dupattas as they walked to work. There was
the blast of muffled horns. The haze lifted the closer we got to
the city and the day burnt through.

At an intersection a beggar child left an imprint of his hand
on the taxi window. The palm print was like an X-ray of longing. I had a bag of fruit which I wanted to give to him. 'Don't
give,' said the driver, his left cheek bulging with paan. 'Not all
are beggars.' Naga looked at me and shrugged. At another intersection I insisted that the driver hand ten rupees to a boy with
twisted limbs. The boy dragged one lifeless leg behind another
as he manoeuvred his crutches, The driver opened the window
slightly but gave the note to a cleaning-wallah who suddenly
appeared. The cleaning-wallah took the ten rupee note, gave
the boy five rupees and started wiping the windscreen. The boy
edged off on his crutches, the money under the stump of one
arm. I wondered if he had a mother and where that mother was.
How they lived. I started to protest, but Naga put his hand on
my arm. 'The money is gone,' he said. 'This is enough.'

The taxi dropped us near the Red Fort and we took a rickshaw
deep into the lanes of Chandni Chowk. We passed stalls of silver

and gold and precious jewels, stalls selling everything for a celebration: sequins and braid, beads and wedding bracelets,
handmade paper and money pouches. We emerged opposite the
Jami Masjid. We'd arranged to meet in Karim's Restaurant. We
were early and we waited, drinking chai and watching the charcoaled chicken and skewered meats coming through from the
kitchen. The smell of meat made me nauseous. Then I saw her
walking towards us. A tall figure with long thin arms and jewelled toes, the pink hibiscus in her hair. The large mouth. The
sea of men parting to make way for her.

Lakshmi took us deep into the old city. Into Paharganj, where
electricity cables hung low over lanes full of children and cows
and dogs. Then we were out into the main bazaar with all the
Buddha and Krishna T-shirts, the bags, the fake-label jeans. We
followed her until she came to a curtained door behind a faded
guest house. She motioned us inside. In the small room we
found a woman and a man and a small boy. The boy, maybe
three years old, was playing on the floor.

'Here,' said Lakshmi.

The incense smoked up, clouding the bright thangkas on
the walls and a large wooden statue of the Buddha. The boy
stood up as we entered and walked straight over to Naga. He
smiled and spoke in Hindi. He was playful and beautiful and
intense and seemed as if he'd been expecting us all along. His
parents stayed silent while Naga opened the cloth bag he'd
brought with him from Dharamsala. He took out three
dholak drums, five alms bowls, five cymbals and three prayer

wheels. He took out some photographs and laid them on the floor.

The child reached for the photographs without hesitation. 'My family,' he said and Naga translated for me. The boy reached for Lama Shastri's old alms bowl. 'Mine,' he said. He returned to the photographs and named each person. Naga smiled and turned to me then looked over at Lakshmi. 'This is the child.'

The boy picked up a photo of Arkay and spoke rapidly, full of excitement. He held it out to me. It was one I had taken. I turned to Naga. 'What did he say?'

Naga leant forward. 'He said that in the past this was his son.'

I raised my camera as the child picked up a dholak drum and Lama's prayer wheel and started to dance.

A studio wall covered in corkboards. A series of prints on a table.

Bhopal, Madhya Pradesh, March 2005

FRANÇOISE

I booked a ticket on the Shatabdhi Express. I caught a taxi to the station. Surjit and Aruna waved me off like family and I told them I'd be back soon.

The taxi driver assured me that he would be driving very smoothly, madam, because the car was new and in good condition. As we turned right out of the colony the driver told me all about his sons, grown now, living in south Delhi out past Gurgaon. 'South Delhi.' He clicked his tongue. 'One day will be as Fatehpur Sikri. You know Fatehpur?'

'Yes,' I said, staring out of the window. 'It's beautiful.' The red-stone city outside Agra, thirsting and abandoned in the desert, left centuries ago.

'South Delhi is dry,' the driver continued, 'yet everyone is moving there. One day the water will be gone and all will leave just like Fatehpur Sikri.' He clicked his tongue. 'What to do? No one learns from history.'

I put on my sunglasses and looked out of the taxi window. 'Maybe some people learn from history,' I said. 'They learn that nothing stays the same. Everything changes, whether they want it or not.'

The taxi driver looked at me in the rear vision mirror and decided to change the subject.

'A son will make your husband proud . . .'

I took a deep breath and smiled. 'Well. I don't have a husband.'

'But the father?'

'Well, he . . .' I hesitated, took another breath. 'He died. Before he even knew he was a father.'

'Madam, I'm most sorry.'

I could see he genuinely was sorry and I thanked him and shielded myself behind the sunglasses. Then I had a sudden desire to tell everything, to tell someone the whole story. 'The baby,' I said. 'Anyway, the baby is a girl.'

'A girl?' The driver gave me a sad look in the mirror, clicked his tongue again and shook his head. We sat in silence all the way to the station.

○

Shahid met me at the studio, two bottles of Kingfisher in hand. 'You've been busy,' he said, pointing to my belly.

'So have you.' He made me laugh, despite myself. Sculptures and maquettes lined the walls. He paced around the room. 'There's more work to do. The touring exhibition.'

'Will I be able to tour?'

'Of course. You will finish your work. You will bring the child with you.'

○

Mist folds over the lakes and mosques and I could frame it like that as if it were the whole picture. As if there were no fishing boats or people walking, no rickshaws, no cars on the bridge. I could frame it that there was only this moment; this pale sound over the water.

I move away from the window. I go through the curtain into the darkroom.

The darkroom is a womb-black space with a red eye in the corner. There's a bright chemical tang. It's a place of high expectation and high disappointment, the place I know best of all. I've learnt to accept everything after the blue click of the shutter; the gap between what I wanted to see and what was actually there. My body is heavy and stiff and it takes a while to ease into this physical work.

There comes a time when we can look at a photograph and not be undone by it.

There comes a day when the work of mourning can begin. I'm not there yet. But last night as I lay in the dark I started thinking of the child as if she were a person. As if maybe things could be different from now on. I started talking to the child, talking to the future as if the future could already talk back.

Lately I find I'm always surprising myself.

I'm back in this city with my camera, drawn to the edges of things. To the edge of the water. To the edge of the factory wall. These edges are always uncertain, always bleeding into something else. Some of the photos are under-exposed, but a good picture is not always about light.

When I'm done and when they're printed I'll put them up around the room on corkboards along with all the rest, because I've learnt that you have to live with the prints for a while. To see how they sound. To trace the underlying patterns and to hear what will last.

When the child is old enough I will show her the collected photos. I will bind them between hard covers. 'These are the stories of how you came to be,' I'll tell her. 'Some were given, some I found. The rest I took myself.' We will open the pages together.

'Take it, it's yours,' I'll say. 'This book. My gift to you.'

ACKNOWLEDGEMENTS

Many people helped me during the long years of writing this book and I want to gratefully acknowledge the following for providing financial assistance: the Unesco-Aschberg Foundation for an International Literature Bursary at Sanskriti Kendra in New Delhi; Asialink, the Australia India Council and the Australia Council for my second residency in India; Shuddha Sengupta and all at the Sarai New Media Collective in Old Delhi for hosting me as Writer in Residence; the Scottish Arts Council for a Writer's Bursary and the Royal Literary Fund in London.

Many thanks to Mr O. P. Jain and all at Sanskriti Kendra for the wonderful times I've had there. To Priti and Sunita Singh and Veena and Ravi Mehta in Delhi for looking after me so well.

To Parminder Sekhon, Neeraj and Mrs Malhotra, Dr Shakuntala Dawesar, Linda Laird, and Phil Brown.

Sathyu Sarangi and all at Sambhavna Clinic in Bhopal. All at the Gas Affected Women's Organization in Bhopal. Moonis Ijlal and family for their hospitality and great kindness during my visits there.

Dr Tamdin at the Tibetan Medical and Astrological Institute in Dharamsala. Gared Jones, Gita Bery and the Tibet Support Group in Delhi. Mr Sharma at the Mehrangarh Fort in Jodhpur.

With thanks to Peter Briggs, Anita Dube, Anna Reid and Ramon Arumi.

Finally, to Peter Bishop of Varuna Writers' House in Australia; my agent Bill Hamilton for his great support and all at Granta, particularly my editor Bella Shand for her creativity and insight.